CHANCE

#4

GAMBLER'S REVENGE

CLAY TANNER

AVON
PUBLISHERS OF BARD, CAMELOT, DISCUS AND FLARE BOOKS

This one's for Richard Potter—on second try.

CHANCE #4: GAMBLER'S REVENGE is an original publication of Avon Books. This work has never before appeared in book form.

AVON BOOKS
A division of
The Hearst Corporation
1790 Broadway
New York, New York 10019

Copyright © 1987 by George W. Proctor
Published by arrangement with the author
Library of Congress Catalog Card Number: 86-91611
ISBN: 0-380-75163-1

First Avon Printing: March 1987

AVON TRADEMARK REG. U.S. PAT. OFF. AND IN OTHER COUNTRIES, MARCA REGISTRADA, HECHO EN U.S.A.

Printed in the U.S.A.

K-R 10 9 8 7 6 5 4 3 2 1

ONE

Chance Sharpe sucked in a long, steadying breath and told himself this was not a matter of life and death. He lied. The next few minutes meant the difference of either resuming his life as a gambler on the Mississippi River or else meeting an abrupt end to that life, dangling from a hangman's noose.

The bailiff's voice rang through the courtroom: "All rise."

With the others gathered before and behind the bar, Chance stood. His gaze traced over the room, alighting on the wide windows that opened onto the freedom outside. After a week waiting behind bars for this hearing, the New Orleans streets looked so close—and so far beyond his grasp.

The sudden urge to dart for the windows and fling himself through the glass panes into the warm light of a late summer's day swelled in his breast. He quelled it. If the need for escape arose, his would come with cool methodical planning and not in a moment of desperation.

Standing beside the gambler, Philip Duwayne reached out and firmly squeezed his friend's shoulder. Chance glanced at the young attorney, sensing that Philip could almost read the thoughts awhirl in his client's head.

"Just a few more minutes and it will be over," Philip whispered.

1

In spite of the reassuring tone, Chance found no comfort in the finality of his friend's words. He ran a finger beneath the collar of his white shirt, his necktie suddenly feeling tight and constricting about his throat.

"It will be over" evoked a gruesome image of the gambler swinging from an executioner's rope, his neck abruptly stretched an unnatural inch or two longer. Dancing in a hangman's noose, branded a murderer, was not the end he would have chosen for his life—especially when he had been neatly framed for that murder.

The irony of his predicament twisted his lips in a cold humorless smile. To be certain, he had not led a spotless life, but to die for another man's act . . .

I'm not going to die. He tried to push the dark thought aside, but it didn't help. Doubt niggled back to haunt him.

He felt like the king of fools. Why hadn't he ridden west to California when he had the chance, instead of returning to New Orleans? Of what concern was a gambler to the law? The phrase "Justice is blind" was deep rooted, and truth often had nothing to do with the way justice's scales tilted. Justice now weighed his claim of innocence against the fact that he had been discovered beside the lifeless body of New Orleans stockbroker Wilson Morehead with the still-smoking murder weapon in his hand.

Morehead had been shot down in cold blood outside Chance's hotel room by a disgruntled young Texan, Gavin Borland. Moving to stop the escaping killer, Chance had lifted Borland's fallen pistol from the floor —which was when every other person on the hotel floor had stepped from his room to find the gambler kneeling over the body, gun in hand.

Jailed by the New Orleans police, Chance had broken out of his cell and trailed Borland across Louisiana and Texas. When he had finally caught up with the killer, however, he found himself on the wrong end of Borland's gun.

He would have died beside the Brazos River had it not been for Clint Borland, Gavin's brother. The older Borland, a duly sworn Texas lawman, had shot his own brother, saving Chance's life. Clint had then ridden back to New Orleans with him, hoping that his testimony would be enough to dismiss the murder changes against the gambler.

The hearing here today would determine if Clint's faith in the legal system had a solid foundation, or was made of sand.

"Having taken..."

The rumble of a man clearing his throat interrupted the words and drew Chance from his thoughts. His gaze shifted to the front of the courtroom. Judge Harlan Turner had taken his seat and was staring over the rims of spectacles, his eyes shifting between the prosecutor and Philip Duwayne.

Turner cleared his throat once more and began again: "Having taken the testimony and evidence into consideration, I have duly deliberated and reached my conclusions."

Chance stared at the snow-haired, black-robed judge. The man's facial expression lent no hint as to what those conclusions were. Nervously, the gambler shifted his weight in his chair.

"While I can not disregard the testimony of those men and women who discovered Chance Sharpe beside the body of the murdered man with a gun in his hand, I do give it little weight." Judge Turner glanced at the prosecutor. "Jesse, as you well know, eyeball witnesses sometimes only see what they think they see, missing important details. In this case the possibility is that the real murderer was running down the stairs while they gawked at the accused here."

Jesse Schuette, the prosecuting attorney, sagged beneath the judge's words.

Turner then looked at Duwayne. "At the same time, counselor, your client found himself in one damning situation. Even in the excitement of the moment, I find it difficult to believe that not one of the twenty men and women who found Mr. Sharpe at the deceased's side didn't hear Gavin Borland darting down the stairs."

It was Duwayne's turn to go limp. Chance's heart tripled its pounding. Turner still gave no indication as to how he would rule.

"Nor would I usually give much weight to the testimony of a brother against his brother. Men—especially those who admit to shooting down their own kin—are far too common these days," the judge continued. "However, in the case of Clint Borland, I can not discount the fact that this man is a duly sworn law officer of the State of Texas. The documents provided by our sister state show him to have a spotless record."

Turner settled back into his chair and stared at Chance. "But the one thing that weighed most heavily in my decision was the fact that you returned to New Orleans, Mr. Sharpe. Only an innocent man would even consider returning to face murder charges when he was so far from the arm of the law. An innocent man— or maybe a crazy man."

The judge's gaze moved to the papers before him on the bench. He shuffled them a moment, then pronounced, "As to the charges of murder pending against Chance Sharpe, they are dismissed."

A long-held breath escaped Chance's lips in a loud sigh of relief. Duwayne's head jerked to his client, a grin beaming from ear to ear.

"Which leaves us with the charges of escaping from

jail and unlawful flight." Turner glanced back at Chance. "Both are serious charges and carry possible prison sentences should a man be convicted of either."

The relief that had coursed through his body an instant ago transformed to panic. Had the murder charge been dismissed only to leave him facing the lesser charges?

"The accused has admitted that he overcame two guards and escaped from jail. However, there are technicalities that muddy the word of the law a bit. Mr. Sharpe had not been charged with any crime when he was incarcerated. As the officers who have testified before this court have repeatedly said, the accused was merely being retained for questioning. In light of that fact, the escape charges are dismissed."

Chance allowed himself another sigh of relief, though with reservations.

"In that light I also dismiss the unlawful flight charges," Turner added. "However, there still remains the matter of public property that was destroyed in Mr. Sharpe's escape."

"Destroyed property, your honor?" Duwayne questioned.

"A matter of a matress within your client's jail cell," the judge replied. "Mr. Sharpe, as he has admitted, set the mattress afire to aid him in his escape. And that mattress was public property."

The attorney's eyebrows arched in question when he looked at Chance.

"For such wanton destruction of private property, I hereby fine Mr. Chance Sharpe five hundred dollars. Pay the bailiff and your client may go free." Turner slammed down his gavel, bringing the case to an end.

Philip started to protest. "Your—"

He was silenced as Chance reached out and grasped

his shoulder. "Let it be, Philip. Pay the bailiff and get me out of here!"

"But five hundred dollars for a bug-infested, straw mattress? It's outrageous. I can't let him get away with that! I'll—" Philip sputtered with indignation.

"You'll pay the bailiff the money, and we'll get the hell out of here before the judge decides to increase the fine," Chance said. "Five hundred is little enough to keep the wheels of justice well oiled."

Philip's lips parted as though he intended to protest further, then he nodded, dug inside his coat for a wallet, and walked toward the bailiff.

Chance grinned. Five hundred dollars was outrageous. But a man in his profession quickly learns when a man sitting across the table from him is holding four aces. Judge Turner held such a hand.

The five hundred was nothing when compared to his spared neck. In this case it was easier to toss in his cards and pay his losses. He walked away a free man and the local officials received enough green to line their pockets and keep them happy.

"I reckon it's time I started back west, Chance," a voice with a thick Texas accent drawled behind the gambler.

Chance turned and faced Clint Borland. The Texan had already tugged a wide-brimmed hat atop his head, which hid the features of his face.

"Going?" He stared at the man in disbelief. "But I've a celebration planned for tonight! You can't go. Not after all you did for me."

"It ain't you, Chance," Clint said, his eyes drifting to the floor. "It just wouldn't set right with me celebrating, what with Gavin dead."

"I understand." Chance reached out, grasped the Texan's hand, and shook it. "Is there anything I can do for you?"

Clint shook his head. "Your men, Captain Rooker and Henri Tuojacque, done seen to everything I'll need —set me up with a pack mule and enough supplies to take me all the way to California and back."

"There's nothing else?"

"Except look me up next time you're down Texas way." Clint grinned, then turned and walked from the courtroom.

Chance watched the man, once more struck by the complicated interior that was hidden by Clint's simple facade. Had they met under different circumstances, they would have become fast friends, of that the gambler was certain. Perhaps in the future they would have that opportunity.

"I *paid* the fine," Philip Duwayne said, coming to his friend's side. "You're a free man."

"Then why are we standing here? I want to see the *Wild Card,* then I've got a night of celebrating ahead of me!"

TWO

Home! The warmth that flooded Chance's breast
stemmed from his surroundings rather than the steaming wooden tub of soapy water from which he stepped.

His cool blue eyes sparked with pride as they traced
around his riverboat stateroom while he toweled his
raven black hair dry. Less than half a year had passed
since he had won the elegant side-wheeler the *Wild
Card* from Tate Browder in a poker game. Yet in that
time, he had come to think of the graceful river lady as
his home.

After the long months spent tracking down Gavin
Borland, it was damned good to be home! If he had
anything to do with it, a month of Sundays would pass
before he was separated from the love of his life for so
long again.

Naked, his lean, muscular body aglisten with drop-
lets of water, he stepped to a mirror hung on a dark-
stained wall above a small table laden with washbowl,
shaving mug, and razor. He worked up a lather in the
mug with a brush and spread it over his cheeks and
neck. The razor's keen edge quickly removed the hint
of stubble shadowing his face, and a splash of brisk
astringent set his cheeks atingle and removed the last
traces of the jail's stench from his nostrils.

Atop his brass bed lay a clean, pressed white shirt
with ruffled collar and cuffs; beside that, a deep
burgundy-hued suit and silk vest to match. Dressing

8

was almost a sensual thrill; clean clothes were a luxury denied him during his week behind bars.

Sitting on the edge of the bed, he tugged on a pair of black, round-toed boots polished to a mirror's shine. For others of professions less hazardous, this might have completed their daily attire. For Chance, whose livelihood came from the roll of dice, the deal of cards, and the spin of the roulette wheel, there were certain accessories that could not be overlooked—that was, if he was to continue living.

He slipped a walrus ivory-handled, razor-honed stiletto into a sheath sewn inside the top of his right boot. Beneath the waistband of his breeches, he tucked a .44 Colt revolver with a sawed-off one-inch barrel. The vest he wore neatly covered the belly-gun's slight bulge. Lastly he nestled a .22 Wesson derringer, hung on a gold watch fob, into a pocket of his west.

Although none of the weapons was meant for distance, they were deadly at the short range that separated men across a poker table. On more than one occasion all three had served to save his skin.

Settling a high-crowned, wide-brimmed hat atop his head, slightly tilted to the right, he moved to a safe hidden behind a painting on one of the walls. Shifting the tumblers through the right combination, he swung the door open and grinned with surprise.

Three bundles of bills, ten thousand dollars in each, were piled inside. Captain Bertram Rooker and the *Wild Card* had made a handsome profit during his long absence. Two of the bundles went into a coat pocket. These would be turned over to Philip Duwayne for deposit in Chance's bank accounts.

The third was broken. Five thousand went into the gambler's wallet and the remainer into another coat pocket to cover the expenses of this evening's celebration.

Chance smiled. Rivermen were a thirsty lot and known to celebrate with their fists as well as their thirsts. Five thousand should more than cover any broken mirrors or shattered chairs and tables that the Hotel Burgundy might suffer before the morning sun rose.

The gambler winked at himself in a full-length mirror as he strode from the stateroom. Outside was a world of regained freedom, and he was prepared for whatever hand life dealt him.

"It's good to have you back, Chance!" Captain Bert Rooker tossed down a shot of bourbon, then grinned from one ear to the other. "The *Wild Card* wasn't the same without you aboard. Things were a mite too quiet."

Chance lifted his glass of champagne to the *Wild Card*'s captain. "I consider that a compliment, Bert."

"Just a fact," the short, square-built man answered in a voice that sounded like gravel grinding together. The captain ran a hand over salt-and-pepper muttonchop sideburns. "Seemed almost like a ghost boat it was so quiet. Not that our passengers minded, you understand."

Chance smiled. Bert Rooker was a river-toughened man who wasn't given to compliments. When one slipped from his lips, he quickly tempered it.

"The rest of the crew appears to be enjoying your return, Chance," said Philip Duwayne, who sat on Chance's right at the table. The young attorney waved an arm around the Hotel Burgundy's casino. "I believe they intend to drink New Orleans dry before the night's over."

"Aye." Bert nodded sternly. "They'll regret it come seven tomorrow morning when we head upriver. You'll never hear so much moaning and groaning."

"You can handle a few headaches." Chance made a

mental note of the *Wild Card*'s departure time; the last thing he wanted to do was miss his own boat in the morning. His gaze then moved around the casino.

At the bar, with a woman on each arm, stood Henri Tuojacque. The handsome young pilot divided his attention between the enticing women and a bottle of champagne. The months Chance had spent in Texas tracking down a murderer had not lessened Henri's roguish streak. The gambler chuckled inwardly. The young Frenchman would one day mature into a taller version of Bert Rooker—if someone didn't slip a knife in his back before then.

However, when it came to working the sticks, as the wheel of a riverboat was often called, there was no better pilot to be found along the Mississippi than Henri Tuojacque. Nor could Chance think of a man he would rather have at his back in a fight, unless it was Bert.

The gambler's gaze shifted to a table set in the corner of the spacious room. There sat Katie MacArt, the riverboat's bartender, with several of the *Wild Card*'s waitresses. While obviously enjoying the spectacle before her, the red-haired beauty was far too proper to join in the revelry.

Not for the first time, Chance wondered what passions lay dormant within Katie's breast. During his months as the *Wild Card*'s owner, their relationship had been strictly business. But one day, he would have to discover just what was hidden behind Katie's cool exterior.

His gaze caught Katie's sparkling emerald green eyes. She grinned and waved. A slight red blush kissed her cheeks and her own gaze rolled shyly to the table when Chance's eyes caressed her beauty beyond the point of a polite casual glance.

The gambler grinned as he turned from the young

woman. Yes, one day he would definitely have to get to know Katie better!

"I'm surprised your crew hasn't run off all the hotel's patrons," Philip said, then sipped from his own glass of champagne.

"They feel the excitement," the gambler said of the casino's customers. "If something happens tonight, they don't want to miss it."

Chance's gaze traveled over the gaming tables. His attention was caught by a pair of jet black feminine eyes that locked to his and lingered there. Curled tresses, as midnight black as those eyes, loosely framed a classical oval face. Lips, as red as rubies, upturned slightly in a silent acknowledgment of his unspoken interest before those enchanting eyes returned to the roulette table.

Philip noticed the direction of his friend's gaze. "Her name's Charlette Blasingame. She's visiting New Orleans."

"Visiting New Orleans?" Chance glanced at the lawyer, then looked back at the shapely woman in a black lace gown as she placed a red chip on the roulette table.

"She and her brother, Howard, are down from Baton Rouge," Philip said. "Rumor has it they're seeking a bank loan."

The attorney explained that the brother and sister had managed to retain their family plantation after the Civil War—barely. With cotton prices hitting rock bottom, they were now faced with the possibility of losing their home and land.

"If he can raise the money, Howard wants to make money crops out of rice and sugarcane. *If* he can raise the money."

"There's a problem?" Chance studied the tall, graceful young woman. She was just as interesting from the back side as she was from the front.

"When it comes to banks, there is," Philip replied. "Bankers are like wolves on the scent of blood. Why help out struggling farmers when there's more to be made by snatching up their land and reselling it?"

Chance needed no further explanation. Carpetbaggers had descended on the South following the war and still preyed on her like vultures. While he had worn Union blue during the War Between the States, he felt no pride in the situation that now existed.

Charlette Blasingame turned slightly and glanced over a creamy shoulder at the gambler. Chance tilted his head toward her. Another smile lifted the corners of the young woman's mouth as she returned to the spinning wheel.

"The Blasingames used to be an influential family," Philip said. "There's the possibility Howard might be able to find a personal loan. But the banks here won't help him."

Chance grimaced as he looked back at his companions. It was a hard future to face, but the South was filled with nothing but hard futures. Men and women did what was needed and survived the best they could.

"She seems to have an eye for you." Bert nodded across the room. "Miss Blasingame just took another gander in this direction."

The gambler lifted his glass and drained it. "Philip, if you don't mind, I think it is time Miss Charlette Blasingame and I were introduced."

"There's a certain magic that seems to hang in the air." Charlette Blasingame leaned on the wrought-iron balustrade and stared over the French Quarter.

"It's called New Orleans." Chance walked from his hotel room onto the small balcony with two glasses of champagne in his hands. He handed one to his lovely companion and lifted the other in a toast. "To the night."

"And the French Quarter." Charlette sipped at the wine. "There's a deliciously wicked feel here. Can you sense it?"

He nodded, moving beside the woman, feeling her warmth as their shoulders brushed. The French Quarter was the oldest section of New Orleans. Here both the French and Spanish had made their city. When the Americans had arrived, they had built their homes and businesses across Canal Street, labeling those who lived in the French Quarter as beneath them.

No respectable man or woman would enter the Quarter during the day. But with the cloak of night, they slipped into the narrow streets to find the pleasures they desired, whether it be a lover purchased for a few hours of passion or narcotic dreams inhaled from an opium pipe.

For Chance, the French Quarter offered casino atop casino in which he might ply his trade while within the Crescent City. It was here he maintained a suite in the Hotel Burgundy to accommodate him. And it was to that suite he had brought this raven-tressed beauty.

"It is magic, isn't it?" Charlette's dark eyes lifted to him as she sipped the last of her champagne.

"The magic I feel is much closer."

Chance took her empty glass and placed it atop the balustrade with his own. He then reached out and lifted her chin with a finger, his lips lightly brushing across the redness of her mouth. "Much, much closer."

There was no moment of coy hesitation when his mouth moved to hers. As his arms slipped around her wasp-slender waist, her lips opened and her tongue met his. Her body willingly melted against his.

"I'm a woman of certain passions, Chance. I've no need to be romanced in the moonlight." A husky, breathless quality filled her voice when their lips parted. Her gaze darted to the balcony's open doors and the bed beyond the threshold. "You brought me here for a reason. I came for the same reason."

With that she slipped from his embrace and stepped into the bedroom, her jet eyes beckoning him to follow. Without a word she turned back the bed's covers, then pivoted and stood facing the gambler.

"Some men prefer removing a woman's clothes, like a child delights in unwrapping Christmas presents. Others prefer watching a woman as she sheds her garments," she said, her eyes remaining locked to Chance's. "You strike me as a man who enjoys watching a woman, Chance."

In truth, he enjoyed both, but Charlotte didn't give him the opportunity to answer. Her arms tucked behind her back, fingers freeing hooks and eyes. Like a dark cloud of lace, her gown slipped from her shoulders, over the womanly flare of her hips, and settled around her ankles.

"It's also easier this way," she said, obviously delighting in his caressing gaze. "No awkward fumblings, no torn buttons."

One by one the layers of her ruffled petticoats and undergarments fell away to join the black gown on the floor. A proud gleam sparkled in her midnight eyes as she slipped a final, thin, silk chemise from her shoulders and eased it downward with taunting languor.

Chance made no false pretense of disinterest: Charlette Blasingame held his undivided attention. Like an evaporating mist the silk cloth slid free to unveil the heavy, slightly pendulous forms of her breasts.

At the crest of each of those creamy swollen mounds perched flaccidly sleeping nipples. Beneath his devouring gaze, the two fleshy buds stirred to life, growing erect until they poked stiffly into the air like ripe, dark cherries demanding to be sampled.

Charlette's nostrils flared and her breasts heaved. He saw a wave of excited gooseflesh ripple across her bare flesh as she guided the skimpy chemise lower, across the fluttering flat plain of her stomach, down to reveal a dark, downy triangle nestled between velvet thighs.

With a sudden wiggle of her hips and two quick flicks of long, shapely legs, she kicked away the chemise and stood naked before him. Unashamed, she turned and strode across the room to the waiting bed.

Chance's gaze followed her every movement, his eyes drinking in the sway of her breasts, the delightful jiggle of her smooth buttocks, the way her sleek calves and thighs tightened with each self-assured step. So cool she was, so regal. The moment was hers, and she knew it.

Reaching the bed, she stretched atop the crisp, white sheets and looked up at the man who stood in the doorway to the balcony. "You are joining me, aren't you?"

Grateful for the shadows that hid the chagrin that washed over his face, Chance realized that every stitch of his own clothing remained on his body. Quickly he tugged off boots and socks and with equal alacrity peeled away his suit and shirt.

Charlette's gaze darted over his nakedness as he stepped toward the bed. A whimper, barely audible in the room's silence, trembled over her red lips when those jet eyes dipped and discovered the full extent of his arousal.

That crack in her cool veneer shattered when he stood at the bed, leaned down, and let his lips teasingly play over the graceful arch of her neck. Upward his lips and tauting tongue slid until his mouth once more covered hers.

Her arms rose and encircled his back. Her thighs

parted in an unspoken invitation. With the increasing pressure of her palms and the playful nip of her fingernails, she pulled him to her until his full weight pressed her into the bed's soft mattress.

Nor did her hands stop there. Slipping down between their cores, she grasped him, squeezed tightly, then guided him forward.

In a single quick thrust, he entered her, sheathing himself in the liquid warmth of her willing body. His own groan of pleasure chorused the lusty moan of passion that pushed from the depths of her throat.

While his hips began a languid dance, his lips and tongue toyed over her dainty earlobes. His hands eased along the velvet of her sides until they slipped upward to cup the heavy mounds of her breasts. Upward his fingers kneaded the pliant flesh, finding and capturing the swollen thickness of her nipples.

Beneath him, her pelvis undulated, matching the rocking movement of his body. Her legs locked around his calves, drawing him even deeper into the moist luxury she offered so freely.

Slowly, each feeding the other's desire with stroking palms and hungry mouths, they rose on the flames of need. Higher and higher their passions flared until each cell of their joined bodies burned.

"My God!" She pulled her mouth from his and cried out in unabandoned pleasure.

Fingernails biting into his back, her hands clawed at his flesh. Her head arched back, and her body went rigid before melting into a series of shuddering quakes.

Unable to contain the mounting fire of his loins, he thrust one last time and joined this magnificent woman in their mutual release.

Together they clutched tightly to each other until the last trembly quiver passed. Only when he flaccidly slipped from her moist harbor did he roll to the side and pull her to him so that her head nestled in the hollow of his shoulder. Soothingly, his palms stroked over the silky texture of her bare flesh.

"I was right," he whispered. "The magic was closer than the city lights." He lifted her chin and lightly kissed her lips. "I think I've fallen under the spell of a sorceress. I only hope you have an incantation that will hold back the dawn."

Charlette pushed to an elbow and returned his kiss. An impish smile touched her lips as she gazed down at him. Teasingly, her fingertips wove through the dark hair sprouted on his chest.

"You've seen all the spells I have to offer. But the night has just begun, and the dawn is still an eternity away. I suggest that we both enjoy the time that remains to us."

Her head lowered; her lips kissed his chest. Downward her mouth worked, until she held him cradled between her cheeks and brought him back to life.

THREE

The narrow streets of the French Quarter glistened with a mirror-sheen of moisture from a brief early morning shower. Overhead thin clouds lazily drifted westward away from a sunrise still a half hour away.

With Charlette Blasingame on his arm, Chance Sharpe stepped from the Hotel Burgundy and requested a cab from the doorman. The gambler surveyed the street as the man briskly stepped to a nearby hack to awaken the cabby drowsing on the driver's seat.

New Orleans reached its morning hour of transition. Here and there carriages rolled down the streets carrying the city's citizens who had overstayed an evening's venture into the French Quarter, back across Canal Street to their lives of respectability. As the last of the night dwellers fled, day workers trundled over the streets atop heavy-wheeled wagons with wide beds laden with burlap bags of fresh oysters and wooden boxes of fish brought in from the Gulf of Mexico.

"Even in the light, there's magic here." Charlette's dark eyes flashed as she took in the predawn scene.

The *pop* of the cabby's whip over the rump of his chestnut mare drew the young woman's attention to the right. A protesting groan sounded from the taxi's spoked wheels as the horse strained against the harness and moved forward.

"But even the most pleasant enchantments must eventually end, Chance."

19

For an instant he saw a shadow of sadness flicker across her face when she turned and lightly kissed his cheek. In the next moment a bright smile touched her lips as she turned and stepped into the cab the doorman held open for her. Nothing else was said while the cabby clucked his mare forward, carrying Charlette back to the American sector of the city.

Nor was there anything else to be said, Chance realized as he watched the taxi slowly disappear down the street. No promises had been made during the night, no lies about the future uttered. A man and a woman had met, touched one another's lives, then parted. Except for delicious memories, there was nothing else.

"Goin' to be another hot one." The doorman's voice brought the gambler from his thoughts. "Air's already as sticky as it was yesterday afternoon."

Chance glanced at the man and then back at the sky. He smiled and nodded, realizing he had paid little attention to the weather. After a week locked behind bars, rain or shine, heat or cold were of little concern. They all felt like freedom to him; all to be savored equally.

"Should I be calling a cab for you, Mr. Chance?" the doorman asked.

Chance slipped a watch from his pocket and thumbed it open. The face read 6:00. He had an hour before the *Wild Card* pulled away from the docks.

Except for a few personal items in his bedroom, everything he needed was on the side-wheeler. After a breakfast in the riverboat's main saloon, he could retire to his stateroom and use the day to catch up on the sleep he had so pleasantly missed during the night. By dusk, he would be ready for the poker tables.

"Give me about fifteen minutes, then have a hack waiting," Chance answered. He lifted a silver dollar from a coat pocket and flipped it to the man.

As he stepped toward the hotel's entrance, the door-man hastened to swing the door wide for him. "Fifteen minutes and a taxi'll be standin' right here for you."

The gambler nodded again and stepped over the threshold.

"Chance!" An urgent voice hailed him from the street. "Chance Sharpe! Chance!"

He turned. A cab bounced from side to side as it raced down the street. Philip Duwayne hung halfway out the window, waving fanatically at the gambler.

"Philip?" He arched an eyebrow high as the cab halted at the curb. "A bit early for you to be out, isn't it, Philip? Or is it a bit late?"

"Both," the young attorney said while he drew a quick gulp of air. He threw open the door to the cab and motioned for the gambler to enter. "Get in, Chance. We've got trouble."

"Trouble?"

"It's your crew." Philip waved him forward once more. "Every one of them—even Captain Rooker—*is in jail!*"

"Would have been charged with inciting a riot if it had been up to me." The desk sergeant grunted in disgust. His gaze shifted between the gambler and lawyer. "But it wasn't. They were merely hauled in for disturbing the peace. Five men taken to the hospital with broken limbs, a paddy wagon and fifteen men called out to pull them in, and all they were hit with was disturbing the peace. Damned lucky I wasn't on duty at the time."

"Can you give us the details of the arrests?" Philip Duwayne asked for the second time, displaying far more patience with the sergeant than Chance had.

"Said I wasn't on duty, didn't I?" the policeman answered with another grunt. "All I know is that bail for the whole lot's been set at two thousand dollars. Pay and you can have 'em back. Don't pay it, and we'll keep 'em."

"Surely there must be reports on the incident," Philip pressed.

"Ain't been filed yet," the sergeant answered with disinterest. "Probably won't be until the graveyard shift comes back on at midnight. Might not be for another couple days. Ain't no concern of mine. Got enough to do keeping up with the men on my shift."

"So move the wheels of justice," Philip muttered beneath his breath so that only Chance heard him.

"Either of you intending to go the bail? If not, move on. I've got a desk full of paperwork that needs doing," the sergeant said.

"I'll pay."

Chance reached inside his coat for his wallet. It appeared that the only way he was gong to find out what had happened was to talk with Bert Rooker and the rest of the crew.

Philip grasped the gambler's arm before he could pull out his wallet. "My legal advice is to leave your men where they are until we can find out exactly what's going on."

"I said that I'd pay the bail," Chance answered with a shake of his head. "I've just sampled the hospitality of a New Orleans jail. I've no intention of allowing my crew to stay in there a minute more than necessary."

A frown creased the attorney's face, and his mouth opened as though to protest. Instead he shook his head. "All right, have it your way. But to keep everything in the light, let me handle this. I am your legal counsel, even if you won't listen to me."

Chance tilted his head in agreement. Philip was right. Two thousand dollars could easily slip through the cracks of New Orleans's legal system and vanish as though it had never existed.

Philip's hand darted inside his coat to withdraw twenty hundred-dollar bills from the money Chance had given him earlier for bank deposit. One at a time he counted them out on the sergeant's desk.

The police officer neatly stacked the bills before him and then placed them into a drawer of his desk. "That should do nicely." He turned and called out. "Charlie, you can release them rowdies form the *Wild Card.*" He then looked back to Philip and Chance. "Will there be anything else?"

"Yes," Philip answered firmly. "A signed receipt!"

The sergeant grunted and quickly scrawled out the receipt and handed it to the lawyer. "Just make sure these men don't get into more trouble—especially during my shift. I won't be as easy on 'em."

"I don't understand." Chance shook his head in disbelief while he turned to an open door that led back to the police station's cells. "I paid for possible damages to the Hotel Burgundy up front. If there had been trouble, I'm certain the manager would have come to me before calling the police."

"I don't know any more than you . . . or our friend the sergeant here. I was just returning home when a messenger arrived at my door. All he said was that Bert Rooker had sent him to find either you or me," Philip answered. "We'll find out what happened soon enough."

The young attorney pointed to the door. Captain Bert Rooker, followed by Henri Tuojacque and the rest of the *Wild Card*'s crew, walked single file from the jail cells. The captain's square jaw was set like a block of granite. His eyes shifted from side to side as though tempting one of the officers to step in his path.

"Chance! Am I glad to see you!" There was no hint of rejoicing or relief in Bert's tone when he noticed his employer. "Do you know what these whoresons have done to us? They've gone and taken—"

"Not here!" Philip silenced the captain. "There are too many ears. An attorney–client relationship is supposed to be confidential."

The lawyer turned to the rest of the men and repeated his order for them to keep their lips sealed. He then looked at Chance. "We need to find a spot with relative privacy."

The gambler pursed his lips and nodded. "There's a cafe down the street. We can pour some coffee into these men and then piece together what happened."

Chance surveyed the tables of his huddled crew. Although they had downed a brewery of liquor last night, it wasn't the effects of hangovers they now suffered. More than half sported angry red lumps on their head, while the other half gazed out through swollen black eyes. It was damned hard to believe that these men had been winning the fight the police had interrupted. Yet the desk sergeant had said that five of their opponents had been sent to the hospital with broken limbs.

The gambler shifted in his chair and looked across the table at Bert and Henri, who nursed cups of steaming chicory coffee. The two had faired no better than the rest of the crew. A knot the size of an egg pushed from the right side of Henri's forehead. Bert's left eye would soon be swollen closed.

"All right, you two," Chance said, "take it from the beginning."

"It wasn't our fault. The bastards tried to stop us from boarding the *Wild Card,*" Henri spoke first. "None of us would have that. Not on your life!"

"From the beginning," Philip repeated firmly. "If I'm going to defend you, I need all the details."

Bert sucked at his teeth and nodded at the attorney. "It was shortly after you left. 'Bout four-thirty this morning, the way I made it. I decided that the celebration had been going on long enough, and if I was to have a crew capable of taking a paddlewheeler upriver, it was time to get the men back aboard my boat."

Chance hid a smile that attempted to climb to his lips. Although he owned the *Wild Card,* Rooker always referred to the vessel as "my boat."

"We had no trouble until we reached the wharf," Henri said, hastening the recounting.

"That's when we saw them toughs lined up in front of the *Wild Card,*" Bert said. "Must have been fifty of 'em if there was one."

"Each one was clutching a club like it was his rosary." Henri's voice betrayed a slight French accent. "Their eyes were afire as though they were just looking for a fight to happen."

Bert took a swallow from his cup and shook his head. "I was walking to the gangplank when a big one comes up to me just as cocky as can be and asks, 'Just where in hell do you think you're goin' old man?' *Old man,* mind you!"

"Then what happened?" Philip urged.

"I told the bastard I was boarding my boat, and he should stand aside," Bert answered indignantly.

"That's when the scum up and tells us all that nobody's going to board," Henri said. "He claims that a Lewis Rapper is the *Wild Card*'s new owner. He says that he and his men are under orders to make certain no one goes aboard."

"That's when I shoved the son of a bitch aside." Bert's fists balled on the table, knuckles turning white. "Said nobody was going to stop me from walking aboard my own boat."

"Two of the others jumped him," Henri added. "And all hell broke loose."

"We had 'em on the run," Bert said proudly. "That's

before the boys in blue arrived and carted us away to jail."

"Lewis Rapper?" Chance's gaze shot to Philip, his mind aswim with dizzying turbulence. Had he heard correctly? Did another man claim ownership of his riverboat? "Owns the *Wild Card?*"

"The officers who arrested us took a look at some paper one of the toughs had," the captain said. "They said the men had a legal right to be there. That all they was doing was protecting private property from vandals like us."

"Legal right to be there?" Chance's confusion grew by the moment. Everything was moving too fast for his brain to grasp. "Philip, do you have any idea what's going on? Who is this Rapper?"

"Lewis Rapper," the young lawyer mumbled as he rubbed a hand over his chin. "The name is vaguely familiar. I can't seem to place it."

"I'll place it!" Chance shoved from the table. The more words he heard, the more befuddled the situation became. It was time for action—his *Wild Card* was at stake! "Give me half an hour, and I'll find this Lewis Rapper and show him who's the legal owner of the *Wild Card!*"

"Chance, sit back down," Philip ordered his client. "Your crew was just released from jail. Until we know exactly what has occurred, I don't want to risk you taking their place."

"What *do* you want me to do? Just sit here and twiddle my thumbs while some son of a bitch I've never heard of before keeps my boat tied to the dock?" Chance fought to control his rising anger. A few moments alone with Lewis Rapper and he was certain he could straighten out the situation.

"That's *exactly* what I want you to do!" Philip stared at this friend and client, his jaw set firm and taut. "You and your men sit right here, have breakfast, and *wait*. Give me some time to get to the bottom of this. If the men at the wharf had a title to the *Wild Card*, then it shouldn't take that long to trace what's happened."

"But—" His frustration mounted with each passing second.

"No 'buts,' Chance." Philip remained adamant. "You released your crew against my advice. You either listen to me now, or find yourself another attorney."

"Philip, this is the *Wild Card* we're talking—"

Philip cut him off sharply. "This is the *law* we're talking about. Damn it, man! Think! Rapper has called the police in on this once. Don't delude yourself into believing he'll hesitate to do it again. If he's somehow making a legal maneuver to gain the *Wild Card*'s ownership, the last thing he wants is the boat's real owner around. Give him an excuse, and he'll see that you're slapped behind bars again! What better place to have you neatly out of his way?"

Chance sucked in a deep breath and dropped back to his chair. His piercing, cold blue eyes glared across the table at his friend. "Damn! I know you're right, Philip. but I can't just sit here doing nothing. It's not my way. You know that."

"Then for this morning you'll have to change your ways, Chance. Give me the opportunity to earn the money you pay me." The edge melted from the lawyer's tone. "It'll only take a few hours for me to trace this. Stay right here with your men. Have breakfast like I said."

The gambler's gaze shifted about the cafe. It suddenly felt smaller, like a cage restraining him. However, this cage had no bars; he could walk out of it anytime he wished. Philip was right about that. If Lewis Rapper somehow managed to have him thrown in jail, he would be tied hand and foot. He had to keep a cool head.

"All right. For now, we'll do it your way, Philip."

"That's all I'm asking." Philip pushed from the table and stood. "Wait here until I return."

The gambler nodded his acceptance again, then watched his friend hasten from the cafe. Like it or not, the fate of the *Wild Card* rested with the young lawyer —for the time being.

FOUR

Chance Sharpe anxiously puffed his way through a long, black, thin sabre cigar. The instant no more than a stub remained, he tossed it into an ashtray, pulled another cigar from his coat and worked his way through it as though he were a smokestack billowing under a full head of steam.

When a glowing, cherry red stub once more protruded from the corner of his mouth, he mashed the smoke out. From a coat pocket he took his watch and thumbed the timepiece open.

A half hour! the gambler snapped the pocket watch closed and dropped it back into his pocket. It felt like days, yet a mere half hour had crept by since Philip Duwayne had left the cafe.

"Chance? Something wrong?" Henri Tuojacque's dark eyes lifted to his friend.

"What isn't wrong!" he snapped at the innocent question, then shook his head in an apology.

"It's the waiting," Captain Bert Rooker said. "It's getting to you."

The gambler ignored the obvious understatement. He glanced around the cafe. His crew was busily devouring a morning meal. His own breakfast sat before him on the table, untouched except for a tepid cup of coffee with one sip gone.

"Maybe you should go for a walk," Bert suggested.

"Take a brisk stroll around the block. Work off some of the steam before it builds too high."

Chance eased back from the table. "I think I'll do just that."

Without another word, he walked out into the New Orleans morning. The hotel doorman's early prediction proved true. The day was hot and muggy. The air clung to him like a soggy blanket.

He ignored it and walked. Movement, even pointless motion, provided the illusion that he was doing something.

Pursing his lips, he tried to lie to himself and failed miserably. Philip's advice for him to stay put was sound; he was certain of that. It was also something he couldn't do. The *Wild Card* was his. If something endangered the riverboat, he had to find out what it was.

And keep my nose clean at the same time, he warned himself. He had no desire to find himself locked behind bars again. His recent stay in jail had been a reminder of the long months of hell he had endured in the Confederate prison in Andersonville during the war.

Uncertain of what course he should take, Chance stopped on a street corner and hailed a passing cab. Swinging the door wide, he slid inside and ordered the driver to the wharf.

He sank back into the cushions and rubbed a hand over his face. He needed to think and sort through all that had happened. Closing his eyes, he carefully went over everything that Bert and Henri had said.

It didn't help. Even thinking it over detail by detail failed to focus the situation. The simple facts were that he was the legal owner of the *Wild Card*. He had won the magnificent lady of the river from her former owner after discovering that the man was cheating at the poker table with a marked deck.

The *Wild Card was* his. He had struggled to keep her

afloat, worked his backside off securing cargo and passengers for her decks. He had even fought off a gang of river pirates who were determined to sink her in the Mississippi's currents.

Hell, I don't even know a Lewis Rapper! What claim could he possibly have to my boat?

None! Chance shook his head. Lewis Rapper, whoever he was, could have no claim to the *Wild Card*.

Yet, the gambler could not disregard the police. Last night they had told Bert that Rapper was the riverboat's owner, that his small army of thugs had a legal right to protect Rapper's private property.

What legal right? He hammered a fist into the taxi's leather cushions. *Damn it! What right could he possibly have? What right?*

That Philip Duwayne was at this very moment attempting to find an answer to that question didn't help. Chance was a man who couldn't leave his life or livelihood in the hands of another, no matter how competent that man was. Since running away from his father's Kentucky home in his early teens, he had depended on but one person for his survival—himself.

A few questions here and there won't hurt, Chance thought. *I'll be careful, stay out of trouble.*

"Whoa!" Outside, the cabby halted his horse. He called back into the hack, "We're here."

Chance stepped out and tossed the driver two silver dollars. "Wait here for me."

Pocketing the coins, the cabby grinned. "You just bought yourself an hour of my time."

Turning, the gambler stared down the wharf. Painted white from stem to stern, the *Wild Card* sat moored in her usual berth at the end of the long wooden pier. A line of men clutching wooden clubs stood before her just as Bert had described. Roustabouts moved up and down her gangplank unloading cargo from her main deck. Passengers, their luggage piled beside them, stood about like lost lambs, uncertain what to do.

Chance ignored the passengers. Other riverboat captains would soon snatch them up for their own vessels. More interesting were the men unloading his craft's cargo.

Someone got the word out quickly, he realized. The cargo owners already had learned of trouble surrounding the *Wild Card* and had received permission to take their goods from the boat. *If this Rapper doesn't intend to sail the* Wild Card, *what is he planning?*

Chance walked along the wharf, unsure exactly what he should do or how to do it once he decided a course of action.

"I'd stop right there, if I was you." A burly bear of a man with a coal pile of a beard covering three-quarters of his face took a threatening step forward as the gambler approached the *Wild Card*'s gangplank. "Ain't no one except those cleared by Mr. Rapper allowed aboard this wheeler."

"Rapper? Who's this Rapper? I want to speak with the boat's owner, Chance Sharpe."

"Ain't nobody named Sharpe here," the man answered. He lifted his club and popped it against his open left palm. "Rapper owns this boat now. If you want to talk to somebody, talk to him."

"Can you point out Mr. Rapper to me?" He glanced from side to side as though attempting to pick out Rapper.

"He ain't here. If you want to talk to him, you'll have to go to his office," the bearded tough replied.

"Office?"

"He's an attorney. Got an office downtown somewheres. Don't know the address."

Chance nodded, storing away the thread of information the man unwittingly gave him. "Do you happen to know by what means Mr. Rapper acquired the *Wild Card?* I had lunch with her former owner yesterday, and he made no mention of selling this vessel."

"Something about back taxes," the man replied, popping his palm with the club again. His eyes suddenly narrowed. "I think you better be moving on. You ask too many questions. I don't like to answer questions. Especially from nosey strangers. Understand?"

Chance glanced at the club, meekly shrank away in his best imitation of a man intimidated by the bludgeon, and tipped his hat to the bearded guard. "I had no intention of overstaying my welcome or causing you any distress. Thank you for your assistance. I will try to meet with Mr. Rapper in his office."

Continuing his Milquetoast performance, he backstepped, then turned and hastily scurried back down the wharf to his waiting cab.

"Where to now?" The cabby stared down from the driver's seat. "Or do you want me to wait for you some more?"

A glance at his pocket watch revealed an hour had passed since he had left the cafe. Chance opened the cab and stepped in, calling out, "Take me back to where you picked me up."

As the taxi rolled forward, the gambler settled back into the cushions. Lewis Rapper was an attorney and taxes were somehow involved in his claim to the *Wild Card*. It wasn't much information but it was a beginning.

Philip Duwayne waved for a cup of coffee as he took the only vacant chair at Chance's table. "Sorry it's taken me so long, but our Lewis Rapper did a good job of covering his trail."

"It *is* a bit past breakfast," Bert Rooker grunted. "Aye, and an hour after lunch."

Philip shrugged at the captain's comment and looked at Chance. "First, I should tell you about Lewis Rapper—"

"He's a lawyer," Chance interrupted. "Somehow taxes are involved in his claim to owning the *Wild Card.*"

Philip's jaw sagged, and his eyes went saucerwide in surprise. "You know? How?"

"That's *all* I know," he replied. "Except that he's got an office somewhere downtown."

Philip shook the incredulous expression from his face and began anew. "Well, there's more—a lot more. I'm surprised that Bert or Henri never heard of Lewis Rapper."

The captain and pilot glanced at each other, then looked at the lawyer with blank stares on their faces. It was Bert who spoke. "Never heard of him 'fore this morning." Henri nodded in agreement.

"He was Tate Browder's attorney," Philip said. "That's why I was certain he was familiar."

"Tate Browder?" a low whistle escaped Chance's lips.

If Browder was even remotely involved in this, it was certain to knot and twist the situation. Browder had been the *Wild Card*'s former owner, a man whose underhanded ways had cost him the riverboat and whose attempts to steal back the paddlewheeler had resulted in his death.

"Browder never let us in on his personal business," Bert commented. "To him, his crew was no more than that—a crew. Never said anything about business."

"Doesn't surprise me," Philip answered. "Browder liked to keep his maneuverings in the shadows. Lewis Rapper was one of his prime movers. The man specializes in completely legal, but more than shady, deals."

Philip then explained that Rapper had been a lieutenant with the Union forces that occupied New Orleans. Originally from Washington, D.C., the Harvard graduate decided to stay in the Crescent City when the war ended.

"You can't even call him a carpetbagger, because he was here before the vultures descended from the North," Philip continued, disgust coloring his tone. "But he's cut from the same cloth. He saw an opportunity to make a fortune off the misery of others and has been taking advantage of it ever since."

Rapper had a couple of thousand dollars in family inheritance, the young attorney said. He quickly increased that amount to ten thousand by buying property that was placed on public auction for back taxes.

"That's what caught Tate Browder's eye, as best as I can tell." Philip paused for a sip of the coffee a waiter brought. "Browder had the capital and Rapper the brains. They were a hellish pair, growing fat and sassy while most of this land starved."

"Browder's been dead for over half a year now," Chance objected. "What connection does Rapper have with the *Wild Card?* How'd he get his hands on her?"

Philip nibbled at his lower lip a moment. "Things start getting a bit murky on that point. When you first came to me to file your title on the *Wild Card,* part of my fee included a title search to ascertain that you had clear legal ownership to your boat. I found nothing clouding the title."

The lawyer paused again as though attempting to sort things in his mind. "Whether it was coincidence or a bit of maneuvering on Browder and Rapper's part, I don't know. But that very day the parrish issued a property tax statement for two hundred dollars due on the *Wild Card.* That statement went to Rapper's office."

"The son of a bitch never contacted me," Chance

said. "I never knew anything about owing two hundred dollars."

"Nor did he contact me," Philip answered. "As things have developed, I'd say this was all part of a plan Tate Browder had for regaining his boat. When Browder was killed, Rapper decided to carry it through himself."

Philip recounted three past due notices for the taxes that were issued while Chance was stalking the murderer Gavin Borland through Texas. "Again these notices were sent to Rapper, who once more failed to pass them on to either you or me."

A cold shiver ran up Chance's spine. The full extent of Rapper's or Browder's, devious scheme was gradually becoming plain. "He got title to the *Wild Card* by paying two hundred dollars in back taxes."

"I'm afraid that's the way it stands." Philip replied softly. "While you were in Texas, the parrish legally seized title and sold the *Wild Card* in public auction."

"It doesn't make sense." This from Henri. "We never saw any police. No official ever came aboard our decks with notice of the seizure."

"That's one thing you can bet I would have noticed," Bert added, his voice filled with gravel. "And I damned sure never saw anyone."

Philip nodded. "That's because all this happened on paper only. I told you Rapper kept his maneuverings in the shadows."

The young lawyer explained that Rapper had apparently greased a few palms so that the fact that the parrish had seized the *Wild Card* never became public knowledge.

"For a few additional dollars, he lubricated the situation even more. Notice of the auction was posted only a few minutes befored the auction actually began. Lewis Rapper was the only man who attended that auction."

"And he bought the *Wild Card* for two hundred dollars!" The words hissed through Chance's clenched teeth. The gambler's elegant river lady was worth between one hundred thousand and one hundred and fifty thousand dollars! "Two hundred dollars! The man stole the *Wild Card!*"

"Morally that's exactly what he did. Legally he purchased possession of the riverboat," Philip said.

"But the whoreson bribed officials. That ain't legal," Bert protested in an outraged sputter. Angry scarlet tinged his cheeks.

"Try and prove it," Chance answered coolly, hiding his own volcanic rage that seethed just beneath the surface of his composed exterior. "It happens every day. Graft and government have walked hand in hand in New Orleans since the end of the war. Anyone in public office looks the other way when money is passed under the table."

"Usually because someone is slipping him his cut under his own table," Henri said glumly.

"Chance is right. We won't get anywhere with alleging bribery. No one's going to testify against a fellow official no matter what he knows. He'd be cutting his own throat," Philip said. "However, I think we have a strong possibility of making a case by going directly at Rapper."

The young attorney then explained that he felt there was a strong foundation for a case of fraud since the parrish never notified the *Wild Card*'s legal owner of the taxes due. Rapper's failure to deliver the tax statement or the three past due notices to either Chance or himself only strengthened the case, Philip said.

"I greased a few palms myself this morning," Philip added. "I filed suit against Rapper and the parrish this morning. A hearing on the case is docketed for tomorrow morning."

Chance merely nodded at the pronouncement. There was nothing else he could do! Lewis Rapper had committed legal robbery—stole the *Wild Card!* Until Philip's hearing tomorrow, his hands were tied.

Controlling his mounting anger, the gambler mentally conceded to wait until Philip had done his best. *Then,* Chance thought, his face going stone hard, *I'll take the reins. And Lewis Rapper will regret the day he ever heard of the* Wild Card *or Chance Sharpe!*

FIVE

Chance Sharpe ducked into the courtroom a step ahead of the bailiff, who closed the doors behind him. The gambler seated himself inconspicuously on a back bench. His gaze quickly took in the scene that filled the hall of justice.

Philip Duwayne stood before the bar and walked toward the judge. From the opposite side of the room a thin man in a conservative black suit and tie and white shirt pushed from behind a table and hastened to the bench.

Lewis Rapper! Chance stiffened. Although he had never seen the man before, he was certain this scarecrow dressed in black was Rapper. Silently the gambler hoped that the old adage that a man who represents himself in court had a fool for a client proved true today.

Chance shook his head. *Scarecrow* was the wrong term; it was too kind.

The gambler estimated the man's height at five foot ten, although his lean frame gave the appearance of a man at least a full six feet. Rapper's dark eyes, sunken features, greasy, slicked-down black hair, and heavily waxed mustache evoked a variety of mental images— none of them pleasing. Spider and weasel stood at the foremost of the gambler's mind.

Rapper's bleached white complexion, the sickly hue of a man who purposely avoided any contact with the sun, added yet another image—walking skeleton. The impression that the attorney strode with one foot in the grave was reinforced by a oily sheen that glistened on the man's face.

Even the gloating smirk that touched the man's lips reminded Chance of oil spreading on water.

The gambler's gaze shifted to Philip Duwayne. The distress he saw on his friend's face sent his stomach plummeting. Although the judge and the young lawyer spoke in whispering tones, both gestured wildly with their arms.

Rapper smoothed his mustache with a fingertip as his smirk spread to a wide grin.

"Your honor, I can't—" Philip's voice abruptly rose. Frustration and anger tinged his tone.

"That's exactly my point, Mr. Duwayne." The judge lifted several legal sheets of paper from his bench and waved them in Philip's face. "You can't continue. Mr. Rapper was not legally bound to inform either your client or yourself of the notices that he received. He was representing the now-deceased Tate Browder. He had not been retained by Mr. Sharpe."

Chance stiffened, dread knotting his stomach. The judge refused to even consider Philip's argument. Had Rapper managed to grease another set of palms?

"Your honor, my client never received notice of the taxes owned—" Philip adamantly continued.

The judge's gavel rose and fell with harsh finality. "Case dismissed. Bailiff, I am retiring to my chambers for fifteen minutes, then I'll hear the next case. Please see that the courtroom is cleared in the meantime."

The judge glared at Philip, leaving no doubt as to whom he wanted out of his courtroom by the time he returned to the bench.

Without a word Lewis Rapper turned, walked to his table, picked up a briefcase, and hurried toward the courtroom's exit. A grin of victory spread across his face from ear to ear. The man's dark eyes met Chance's gaze as he passed. The gambler noted no flickering glimmer of recognition on the attorney's face.

The urge to take Rapper's neck between his fingers and quickly end the man's claim of ownership to the *Wild Card* was almost overwhelming. As much as he would have enjoyed the task of crushing the man's throat, Chance forced himself to remain in his seat. Killing Rapper would solve nothing, no matter how pleasant it might be; his riverboat would still be part of Rapper's estate.

Chance glanced back across the bar. The bailiff stood near as Philip angrily stuffed a fistful of paper into his own briefcase. Mumbling curses beneath his breath, the young lawyer stalked toward the door.

Chance stood as his friend reached his position. "I gather that was Lewis Rapper."

"Chance, I didn't know you were here. Did you hear the judge?"

"I heard everything." The anger that had burned in his breast since yesterday morning was slowly cooling, transforming to icy determination. "Was that Rapper?"

"One and the same." Philip motioned the gambler from the courtroom ahead of him. "I think the bastard got to the judge."

"He looked right at me, Philip," Chance said, ignoring his friend's last comment. If the judge had been bribed, it was too late to do anything about it. "He acted as though he had never seen me before in his life."

"I doubt that he had," Philip answered. "For what he's done, Rapper had no need to meet you. Chance Sharpe is just the name of the *Wild Card*'s former owner to him. A signature on a title—nothing more or less."

Chance stroked his throat as they walked toward a

flight of stairs that led to the courthouse's ground floor. "That might be in my favor. Could make things easier."

"Chance, what happened in there today isn't the end of this. I'll appeal, file again and find a judge who'll—" Philip stopped abruptly and stared at his friend and client. "Make things easier? Chance, what do you mean? You aren't considering going after Rapper, are you?"

"You mean doing bodily harm to Mr. Lewis Rapper?" Chance asked without a trace of humor in his tone. "Believe me, I've thought of it. And discarded the idea."

"Then what's on your mind?"

He shook his head and sucked at his teeth. "I don't know. But Rapper isn't going to get away with legal robbery. You have my word on that, Philip. I might have my back against the wall now, but if it's the last thing I do, Lewis Rapper will pay dearly for what he's done."

Philip stared at the gambler. No doubt flickered in his eyes. If Chance Sharpe had a code that he lived by, it was summed up in the term *fair play.* If he, or a friend, were wronged, Chance wouldn't be stopped until the wrong was righted.

"Rapper hasn't won yet," he continued. "Don't know how, but I'll get the *Wild Card* back from him, plus enough to make certain he never tries anything like this again."

"Chance," Philip started, then paused. He opened his briefcase, dug within, and pulled out a yellow sheet of paper that he handed to the gambler. "I think you'd better read this."

Chance unfolded the paper and read a bold, black banner emblazoned across the top of the handbill:

TO BE SOLD IN PUBLIC AUCTION—THE RIVERBOAT *WILD CARD*

Beneath the banner and a line drawing of a stern-wheeler, was the announcement that Lewis Rapper would hold an auction open to all the public sixty days hence. Opening bid for the riverboat was posted at ten thousand dollars.

"Son of a bitch!" He crushed the handbill into a tight, crumpled ball. "Every riverboat line and half the independents will be at that auction. They'll be like a pack of wolves after a wounded deer!"

"Sixty days isn't much time, Chance." Philip stared at his friend. "Even if I can get another hearing, the wheels of justice turn slowly..."

"Two months is two months," he replied, his mind racing. "If it's all the time I have, then I'll make do with it."

"What can you possibly—"

"I don't know." Chance tossed the balled handbill aside, wishing it were a rock he could hurl through a windowpane. "The first thing I have to do is find out just who this Lewis Rapper is and what he's made out of."

"That in itself could take two months," Philip answered.

"It'll take two days, no more," he replied, his voice coming cool as an Artic breeze. "In that time I want to know everything there is about Lewis Rapper. Everything! Even how many times a day the man relieves himself!"

SIX

Philip Duwayne's housekeeper Clarice cleared the dining table, then brought a silver tray laden with two pots of coffee and five cups. Philip waved her away as she began to serve her employer and his four guests.

"We can serve ourselves, Clarice," Philip said, then waited until the housekeeper left the room before turning to Chance. "Are we ready to piece together what we've discovered?"

"Probably not, but two days from sixty leaves us with only fifty-eight until Rapper places the *Wild Card* on the auction block," Chance answered. "We can't waste any more time."

The gambler's cool blue eyes traveled around the table, briefly glancing at the faces of his companions gathered in the hope of regaining a riverboat that had been legally stolen from them. Bert Rooker and Henri Tuojacque nodded when his eyes met theirs. Katie MacArt's emerald-hued eyes no longer sparkled with gaiety, but were set with hard determination. Philip Duwayne also returned his client's gaze with a nod.

In spite of the gravity of the gathering, Chance felt the warmth of pride swell in his chest. During the few short months that had passed since meeting these four, a deep-rooted friendship had grown between them. He could not ask for a better group at his side.

"If there's no objections, I'd like to start off." Philip

cleared his throat. "I employed two ex–police officers to assist in our research into Lewis Rapper's life."

Chance lifted an eyebrow in surprise, and then smiled. His own "research" had been conducted through less open avenues. He would have never considered former law officers. Philip's was a good choice. Policemen, even those retired from the force, often knew what skeletons to rattle in what closets when they needed something fast.

Philip stood and walked to where his briefcase sat in a corner of the dining room. He extracted a file from the leather bag and returned to his chair. He flipped quickly through two pages before stopping.

"The first part of this confirms the information I had already obtained—that Rapper came from Washington, D.C., decided to remain in New Orleans after the war, and was Tate Browder's attorney of record," Philip said. "After that it becomes a bit more interesting."

According to the report, Rapper had done more than just invest Tate Browder's money in various land deals. His own bank accounts had grown larger each day from ill-gotten profits he reaped from the misery of others.

"Buy land and business concerns for past due back taxes and sell them for a quick profit. It's the way he's operated since arriving here," Philip said. "There was nothing personal in the way he snatched up the *Wild Card*. It's merely Rapper's method."

"That makes me feel a *hell* of a lot better, Philip." Chance rolled his eyes. "Knowing Rapper wasn't out to get me personally really takes a weight off my shoulders."

Philip smiled sheepishly at the sarcasm, then cleared his throat again. "While it might not allow you to sleep better tonight, it does give us an insight into the man we're dealing with. To Rapper the *Wild Card* is merely another piece of property from which he hopes to make a profit. He has no other interst in it. Nor do I expect he'll pay any more attention to it than he will to several deals he has in the works."

"You didn't go up against his army of toughs." Henri gingerly touched the lump on his head. "If you ask me, he's taken quite an interest in our riverboat."

"I won't argue with that." Bert peered out from behind a swollen black eye.

"The crew you ran head-on into at the wharf are part of his standard operating procedure," Chance said to the captain and pilot as he revealed a portion of what his own investigations had uncovered. "They work for a man named Galt Ferris. Whenever Rapper moves in on a piece of property, Ferris and his men are called in to protect it."

"Which means they're ready at Rapper's beck and call," Henri said.

Chance nodded. He recognized the possibility that fists, maybe even guns, might be needed to regain his side-wheeler. "If required, we'll deal with them when the time comes."

Bert grunted. A sparkle of anticipation flashed in his eyes. "Time won't come soon enough for me. I don't like no man stoppin' me from boardin' my own boat."

"I thought we were here to find a means of dealing with Rapper without the use of force." This from Philip.

"We are," Chance assured the young attorney. "But we can't overlook the possibility that Rapper might not react in a civilized manner."

"A wise man once said that violence is the last course of fools," Katie spoke up in a voice that betrayed her Irish heritage and spirit. "While we may be rational, we might stand facing a fool, Mr. Duwayne."

Philip cast a dubious glance at his companions, then

looked back at the report on the table. "As Chance said, we deal with Ferris and his men if and when the need arises. For the time being, we should get back to our reason for meeting here—Lewis Rapper."

"Agreed." Chance tilted his head, indicating the lawyer was to proceed.

"My investigators indicate that while Rapper has made a small fortune during his brief stay in New Orleans, he is far from being in a stable financial situation," Philip began anew. "He's a man that lives right on the edge of his monetary capabilities."

The lawyer recounted Rapper's purchase of an old plantation and the expensive furnishings he was currently importing from Europe. In past months Rapper had developed a reputation for entertaining New Orleans society with large lavish parties in his home.

"Aye!" Katie nodded. "I've friends, maids who attend the wealthy. It seems that Mr. Rapper is searching for a bride."

Chance's eyes widened. After having seen the oily attorney, he found it difficult to believe any woman, no matter how homely, would give Rapper a second look.

"The rumors are that Mr. Rapper is a man of fickle tastes. He wants to ensure that his future bride comes from a suitable family who will ensure his social status here in New Orleans," Katie continued. "It's also said Mr. Rapper may have a long wait before finding a wife. I understand the man's ugly as sin itself."

"There's mention here that Rapper may be seeking a wife," Philip said as he flipped through the report. "It also says that the families he's courting aren't impressed. While the report makes no mention of his physical appearance, it does say his rather precarious financial position is less than attractive to the families he's been entertaining."

Chance listened, realizing that the majority of New

Orleans's elite were in dire financial straits themselves. Although their names might still have weight in the Crescent City, the war had left most of them with little more than the property they owned.

A father might be willing to sacrifice a daughter in marriage to bolster his monetary base, even to a man like Rapper. Without the assurance of ready cash, they would allow themselves to be wined and dined at lavish parties while never giving such a man serious consideration as a possible son-in-law.

Nor was a woman above agreeing to such a match if it would ensure protecting her family and their lands.

Cold dread infused Chance's body. He remembered Charlette Blasingame and the night of magic they had shared. He silently hoped that she and her brother Howard had found the loan that had brought them to New Orleans. The thought of such a magnificent woman forced to marry a man of Rapper's ilk knotted the gambler's stomach.

"The men in my employ also uncovered that Rapper has only ten thousand in hard cash in his bank accounts." Philip's voice brought Chance from his thoughts. "Rapper's cash is normally tied up in land or stock speculation. Most of this back East and apparently unsuccessful. He's lost as much as he's made during the last six months."

"The bastard's got a greedy streak in him." Bert grinned.

"More important, Rapper has very little operating capital at the moment." Chance poured himself a cup of coffee and took a sip. "That means he's vulnerable. Now all we need is a method to get at that soft spot."

"Horse—" Henri started.

Philip interrupted. "I think you should also know that Rapper has sent out letters to all the major shipping firms on the river, announcing the *Wild Card*'s auction."

"Apparently he's afraid his handbills aren't enough to draw in the big bidders." Chance contained the curses that rose in his throat. Pushing aside his anger, he looked back at Philip. "The man's short on hard cash—does that report mention any other weaknesses? Liquor? Women? Anything we can work with? Anything at all?"

Philip glanced over the final page of the report and shook his head. "The rest is just a list of his Eastern deals that have fallen through. As sly and slippery as Lewis Rapper is here, he seems to be a rather reckless gambler when it comes to his East Coast investments."

"He *is* a gambler!" Bert stared across the table at Chance. "That's what Henri was trying to tell you."

Chance's head jerked to the young pilot, his forehead furrowed in question.

"Horses," Henri said. "You said that you wanted to know his weaknesses. It's horses. It's about all Bert and I could find out about the man."

"There is mention here of Rapper raising horses"— Philip glanced back through his report—"but that's all."

"He gambles a little," Bert spoke up again. "But nothing serious, except for horses."

Chance's mind raced, wheels turning; a smile uplifted the corners of his mouth. Gambling was something he understood. Although he would have preferred facing Rapper across a poker table, he might have, just might have, discovered the bait needed to ensnare a legal eagle.

"There's no reason to be agrinnin'," Bert said with a shake of his head. "Rapper ain't nothing but a winner when it comes to horses."

The gambler arched a questioning eyebrow.

"He owns a three-year-old colt named Legacy," Henri explained. "The colt's had twenty starts and twenty wins. From what we could find out, Legacy is the fastest thing on four legs in Louisiana."

"This last month Rapper's only been able to drum up one match race for the colt," Bert added. "Can't find any one foolish enough to go up against his horse."

Chance's smile grew. He knew the bait; now he had to construct the trap. A barrage of possibilities assailed his brain. Discarding the obvious jetsam, he selected bits and pieces for his snare.

"You're still smilin' like a jackass, Chance," Bert said. "Didn't you hear Henri? This colt is the fastest thing on four legs in Louisiana."

"At least at a mile," Henri said. "He hasn't been beaten."

"There are more states in the Union than Louisiana," Chance answered, his voice that of a man whose thoughts traveled elsewhere. "Other horses."

"Chance?" Katie stared at the gambler. "What are you thinking?"

"I'm not sure." He held the pieces he needed; now all he had to do was juggle them into their proper places. Two men could play Rapper's game. If one man could commit legal robbery, so could another.

"Chance?" Philip leaned toward his friend. Concern lined his face.

"The name's . . ." Chance's thoughts stumbled as he grasped for a name that would be easily remembered. "William Forrest."

"William Forrest?" Philip's concern increased. "What are you talking about?"

"His mind's snapped," Bert grunted and shook his head.

"Rapper would never consider doing business with a man named Chance Sharpe," the gambler answered.

"He might not know what I look like, but he does know the name."

"I still don't see what you're getting at." Philip continued to stare at his friend.

"I want you to change my name, Philip. Legally that is. You can do that, can't you?"

"Certainly." Philip's slow nod said that he still didn't understand what rushed through the gambler's mind. "Fill out a boilerplate form and pay the fee is all it takes to change a name. One moment you're Chance Sharpe and in the next you're William Forrest. Hell, it doesn't take much more to make you a legal business in the State of Louisiana!"

Chance completely missed the exasperation in the young lawyer's voice. "Business! That's an even better idea, Philip! William Forrest, a sole proprietorship with yours truly as the owner. Just make certain that the name is William Forrest, nothing more or nothing less. That's important. The name must be William Forrest. If you need to specify a business activity, list William Forrest as a racing stable. When can you have it done —officially, that is?"

"Tomorrow," Philip replied without thinking, then asked, "Chance, don't you think you should let us in on what you're thinking?"

Chance mentally edged the pieces into place too rapidly to pause and explain. "William Forrest also needs a place to live. Not here in New Orleans, that might be too obvious. Baton Rouge would be close enough and might be less suspicious to Rapper."

The gambler glanced back at Philip. "The Blasingame plantation? Does it have a stable?"

"The Blasingame place?" Philip sputtered, his confusion deepening with each passing second. "What do the Blasingames have to do with this?"

"Nothing really, except I think I can prevent a disastrous marriage while trying to save the *Wild Card,*" he answered, recalling his earlier vision of Charlette Blasingame forced into wedding a man like Lewis Rapper. "Philip, I want you to locate Howard and Charlette Blasingame. If they have a stable, offer them a loan at no interest in exchange for the lease of their home for the next two months."

"You're going to give them a loan?" Philip gawked at his client.

"If it's within reason. If it's too high, then find another place to rent. Just make certain that it has a stable," Chance replied. "Also make certain that it is generally known that William Forrest is buying both house and land. Henri, I want you to assist Philip in any way you can."

Henri shrugged, apparently as confused as the young lawyer.

"There's that William Forrest again," Bert said, glancing at his companions around the table. "Who is this William Forrest?"

"To all of us in this room, it's me," Chance said. "But as far as the rest of the world is concerned— especially Lewis Rapper—William Forrest is a wealthy horseman from Louisville, Kentucky, on his way to Baton Rouge to begin a breeding farm."

Philip's mouth sagged open. "Chance, isn't this getting a mite elaborate?"

"It has to be. It's the only way it will work." His gaze shifted to Katie. "I'd like all of you to meet Katherine Forrest, William's sister." The gambler held out an arm to the redhead.

"Katherine Forrest?" Katie blinked twice before her eyes narrowed.

"William has sent you to Louisiana ahead of him to make certain that his new home is in order. Of course, you'll frequently come to New Orleans, and you'll meet Lewis Rapper. Philip will see to that."

"Me?" Philip sank back into his chair.

"Tomorrow Katie will go on a shopping spree and buy a wardrobe befitting a young Southern lady of wealth. Your job is to escort her to all the right social functions—especially those where she is certain to be introduced to Lewis Rapper," Chance explained, then looked back at Katie. "And your task is to make sure that Rapper knows about your brother William and the breeding farm."

He paused and smiled at the bewildered woman. "You can do it, I know you can. Prepare him well, Katie. I want Rapper chomping at the bit to meet William Forrest when he finally arrives in New Orleans about a month from today."

Katie swallowed and nodded. "If that's what you want, Chance. But what do I know about my new brother?"

"He looks like me." Chance grinned and shrugged. "Other than that, you'll have to play it by ear. Just be sure you keep track of everything you tell Rapper. You'll have to fill me in once I'm back."

"You're going somewhere?" Philip's tone was that of a man gone numb.

"Bert and I are, as soon as I can send a telegram," he answered.

"And where might we be agoin'?" the captain asked.

"At least to St. Louis," the gambler replied. "I should get the answer to my telegram there. After that —well, we'll have to wait and see what the answer is."

Henri shifted forward in his chair and looked Chance in the eyes. "You've got a plan, Chance. That much is plain. Mind telling us what it is?"

The gambler drew a deep breath and slowly released it. "When Bert and I get back, I'll tell you everything.

Until then, the less you know the better. You'll have less chance of saying something that might run us aground on a sandbar."

His friends' expressions said that they weren't happy with his answer, but they accepted it. For now, that was the way it would have to be. Each had their roles to play, and that was enough.

In truth, Chance realized, that might be more than enough. The elaborate groundwork Katie, Henri, and Philip would lay for William Forrest's arrival might all be in vain. Until he received an answer from his old friend Shakey Haygood, he might not even have a plan!

SEVEN

A waiter in black suit and tie swung a tray down from his shoulder and placed it atop the table. "Gentlemen, the refreshments you ordered. Captain Smead, coffee, hot and black."

The man served Efram Smead first. Although others of the seven seated around the poker table might be more rich or influential, the waiter was fully aware of Smead's status as captain and owner of the *Missouri Comet*. The six other men might tip the waiter, but Smead paid his salary.

"And the same for you." The waiter poured a steaming black stream into a porcelain cup, filling it to the rim, then placing cup and saucer in front of Chance Sharpe.

The gambler took a sip of the scalding brew, then set it aside to cool. He reached into a breast pocket to withdraw the last of five saber cigars he had placed in the coat last evening.

While the waiter served the remaining five men at the table, Chance bit off one end of the cigar and lit the other. He inhaled deeply and slowly released the blue smoke from his lungs in a thin stream. A cool breeze drew his gaze to the open forward doors of the sidewheeler's main saloon.

Outside, the inky blackness of night gradually transformed to the murky gray of predawn. Beyond the bow of the two-hundred-foot riverboat, he discerned ripples rolling across the muddy surface of the Mississippi River.

The clink of a stirring spoon against the side of a cup brought the gambler's attention back to the table. Richard Sheldon, a Missouri banker on the captain's left, heaped two spoonfuls of sugar into a cup, then eagerly slurped at the overly sweet mixture.

To Sheldon's left sat a jovial tobacco merchant, Willard Carson, who shared a last round of foaming beer with Gil Wagoner, a St. Louis shoe manufacturer seated at Carson's left elbow.

"I'll hate to see this trip end, my friends." Jeb Muckaroy spoke between cooling blows across his own cup of coffee. "Can't remember a more enjoyable journey on the river."

Muckaroy, a tall, lanky, adopted Texan, grinned at his companions. The man traveled north to his native Kentucky to convince two brothers to return with him to the Lone Star State. Since the end of the war, the United States had discovered a taste for beef. Muckaroy, like many Texans, had turned to ranching and could talk for hours on end about the profits to be made from selling beeves on the hoof.

"I don't doubt that. You've won consistently since we pulled away from New Orleans." This came from Stuart Grant, the last man seated at the green felt-covered table.

Like Chance, Grant was a professional gambler. Unlike Chance, Grant's luck had run sour the past four nights, and he was a heavy loser. Chance estimated the man had lost close to a thousand dollars.

"All things must pass," Smead answered the Texan. "In another hour or two, the *Missouri Comet* will be docking in St. Louis, and we'll all go our separate ways. But before that, we have time for one last hand of poker together." The captain raised his coffee in a mock toast. "May it be an interesting one. Chance, I believe it's your deal."

"Five card draw, jacks or better to open." Chance raked in the cards at the center of the table as the waiter lifted the tray from the table. He then tossed a dollar down. "Ante up, gentlemen."

Something's wrong! Caution jolted through the gambler as he neatly stacked the deck and shuffled them three times.

As certainly as a diamond cutter knows the rough stones with which he works, Chance's fingertips intimately read the stack of cards in his hands. The deck was short. Three cards were missing.

Three, he assured himself with a brush of his right hand as he passed the deck to Grant for the cut. One of the other players had held out three cards. *And I missed it!* He realized that the cards had been slipped from the table during the momentary diversion the waiter had caused.

Who? His gaze shifted over the faces of his fellow players as he dealt the hand. Which one: Smead, Sheldon, Carson, Wagoner or Muckaroy?

He never considered Grant. Although the man had the needed skills to conceal the cards, he wasn't foolish enough to attempt such a ploy. Not with another gambler sitting at his elbow.

The gambler continued to survey his opponents as he dealt himself the last card and lifted his hand from the table. A pair of jacks, a ten, seven and deuce filled the fan in his left hand.

"Pass," Captain Smead said.

His lack of openers was repeated in sequence until the betting moved around the table to Chance. For a moment, the gambler considered folding and passing the deck to the captain for a new deal. He discarded the idea. If he wanted to smoke out his dishonest companion, he had to bait a trap.

"I'll open for twenty." Chance lifted two ten-dollar bills from the stack of money neatly piled before him and tossed it atop the seven-dollar ante at the middle of the table.

"I'll call." Captain Smead matched the twenty.

As did Richard Sheldon. Willard Carson added another ten, and Gil Wagoner folded. The Texan Jeb Muckaroy saw the thirty, and Stuart Grant kicked the bet up to fifty.

Chance caught himself before he arched a surprised eyebrow. As well as luck, had Grant lost his senses? Such heavy betting so soon normally drove off players holding marginally decent hands.

Or have I misjudged Grant? Chance reconsidered his earlier conclusion about the gambler as he sweetened the pot with the needed thirty to remain in the game. Had Grant's heavy losses driven him to desperation? He might have pulled the three missing cards.

To Chance's surprise, Captain Smead and the remaining players called the bet. Now only the shoe manufacturer could be considered an innocent bystander—Wagoner was out of the game.

"It's your bet." Chance glanced at Grant. "How many cards?"

"Two." Grant tossed away two of the blue-backed Steamboat playing cards and picked up the two dealt him.

That Grant had asked for only two cards did not eliminate him from suspicion, Chance thought as he discarded three cards and dealt his three replacements. A man with three cards in his pocket could make the switch at any time.

Both Smead and Sheldon took two cards while Carson and Muckaroy asked for three. The draws gave Chance no hint as to the identity of his cheat.

A glance at his own draw brought no improvement to Chance's pair of jacks. When Grant began the betting again with twenty-five dollars, Chance folded.

Captain Smead bumped the bet to fifty. And so the betting proceeded around the table, making the total a hundred and twenty-five when it reached Stuart Grant again. The gambler met the bet and upped it by another fifty.

All the while, Chance's gaze moved from player to player. None of the men made a move for the concealed cards.

"Too steep for me." Captain Smead tossed down his cards in disgust. "Not a bad hand, either; just not that good."

The banker Sheldon saw the bet as did the tobacco merchant Carson. Muckaroy dropped in another fifty atop the fifty needed to see Grant's raise.

Chance tensed. Grant coughed, his hand darting to a pocket. The man came up with only a white handkerchief.

So intent was he on watching his fellow gambler that he almost missed the hint of barely discernible blue between two spread fingers as a player across the table pulled a pouch of tobacco from his coat to fill a pipe.

Chance held himself. While one man played a dishonest game, the others bet their money in earnest. He would wait until the hands were face up on the table before exposing the culprit.

After another glance at his cards, Grant called the Texan, as did Sheldon. Carson raised another fifty. The remaining players saw the raise. The showdown had come!

"A full house," Carson announced as he spread three aces and two kings on the green felt.

"Beats the hell out of my three eights." Muckaroy tossed his hand to the table.

"And my two pair." Sheldon threw his cards down with a shake of his head.

"Lady Luck is like any other woman, Chance." Stuart Grant glanced at his fellow gambler and shrugged. "She's fickle as they come."

Grant fanned his hand faceup on the table. Three fives and a pair of nines.

"Thought certain I had it this time." Grant shrugged again. "Just hasn't been my time, I guess."

"Looks that way." Willard Carson the tobacco merchant beamed. "Biggest pot tonight, and it's all mine."

Chance waited until the man reached out with both hands to scoop the piled winnings to him. The gambler's right hand tugged at the watch fob that ran to his vest pocket. A silvered, double-barreled, .22 Wesson derringer sprang into his palm.

Before any of the others at the table even noticed the weapon, Chance's thumb jerked back the hammer. His arm shot out, aiming the deadly little pistol directly between the merchant's hazel eyes.

"Unless you'd like a window opened in your skull, I'd leave that money exactly where it is." Chance's words came cold and harsh, leaving no doubt that he was quite willling to pull the hideaway trigger if necessary.

"Wha-what?" Carson sputtered, the pipe clenched between his teeth falling to the table.

"Chance?" Captain Smead brought a .45 out from his coat and aimed the gun at Chance. "Overreacting a might, aren't you? Why don't you put that pop toy down and let Mr. Carson here collect his winnings?"

Chance's eyes narrowed, never leaving the tobacco merchant, even when he heard Smead's weapon cock.

"Make a move, Carson, and I'll empty both these barrels."

Carson's outstretched arms hoverred above the green bills mountained at the center of the table.

"Captain, if you'll have Mr. Sheldon look in Carson's right pocket, you'll find three cards our friend here has been holding out."

The steamboat captain nodded to the banker. Cautiously Sheldon reached out and dipped a hand into the merchant's coat pocket. He extracted a tobacco pouch with three blue-backed cards nestled beside it. Sheldon tossed down a three, a deuce, and a five.

"The son of a bitch has been cheating us!" This from Jeb Muckaroy. "If we were back home, we'd string the bastard from the nearest tree!"

"An appropriate measure." Smead swung his pistol from Chance to the merchant. "But it's damned difficult to find trees growing in the middle of the Mississippi."

"What do you intend to do with him?" Sheldon looked up at the captain.

Chance carefully eased the hammer of the derringer down. With Smead covering the man there was no need of the weapon; he tucked it back in his vest pocket. A cold shiver worked along his spine when he turned to the steamer's owner and captain.

While aboard a paddlewheeler, there was but one law, judge, and jury for those who transgressed a riverboat's rules of conduct—the captain. Smead's dark glowering expression said that Carson's punishment had been decided.

"The way I see it, Mr. Grant won the pot fair and square. Take your winnings, Mr. Grant." Smead tilted his head toward the gambler.

Grant hastily raked the bills from the table into his pockets.

"As for Carson—throw him overboard!" Smead handed down the sentence.

Sheldon, Wagoner, and Muckaroy needed no further word. Pushing from their chairs, they jerked the man to his feet and dragged him from the main saloon to the guard walk outside. Holding the tobacco merchant by his arms and legs, they swung him back and forth three times, then heaved the screaming man overboard. His cries ended abruptly as he hit the water below like a sack of potatoes.

"Can he swim?" Sheldon asked, his eyes wide when he turned to the captain.

"Doesn't matter." Smead called down to the lower main deck. "You two up here on the double. I want the Ohio stateroom cleaned out immediately. Toss all the passenger's personal items over the side!"

Two roustabouts came on a run. Smead watched their every stride, never looking back to the man he had ordered tossed overboard.

Chance did glance back. Carson swam, arms stretching out and feet kicking wildly. Whether the man had the strength to make it to shore was not the gambler's concern. Smead had dealt out his personal version of river justice fairly and quickly.

"He's swimmin'," Jeb Muckaroy said with obvious disappointment. "A tree would have been better."

"Gentlemen, I have duties to attend." Smead turned to his companions. "If you'll excuse me, I must get to the pilothouse. My turn at the wheel."

With a last glance at the swimming merchant, Chance walked back into the main saloon. He took his money from the table and placed it inside his wallet. Although he had not won the last hand, the bundle had gained a handsome heft during the night's play.

"Chance, I want to thank you for what you just did," Stuart Grant said at his side.

"It was nothing. You'd have done the same for me."

"I'd like to think so," Grant replied. He awkwardly shuffled from one foot to another. "Anyway, I just wanted to tell you that I owe you one. Someday when we meet again, I hope to make it up to you."

Chance nodded and tipped his hat to the man before turning and walking down the row of doors that lined the left side of the main cabin. He didn't doubt Grant's word. The Mississippi, for all its vastness, was a small world. He and the gambler might very well meet again and the circumstance could be reversed.

Reaching a door marked *Vermont,* Chance opened it and entered. Bert Rooker stood shaving in front of a mirror hung on the wall. From the swollen appearance of his eyes, it was obvious he had arisen within the past half hour.

"I know different men have different ways, but I don't see how you do it." Bert shook his head. "For most, the sunrise is time to meet a new day, and you're just getting to bed."

"Like you said, different men, different ways." Chance sat on the edge of the stateroom's lower bunk. When Bert had toweled his face clean, he tossed his wallet to the captain. "Add that to our funds. We'll need it before we're through."

Bert extracted the money and quickly counted it. "Whew. That makes three thousand you've won since we left New Orleans. For the past two weeks I've had a hell of a time just keeping myself sane, and you've won a small fortune." The captain shook his head in amazement.

"It's what I do to keep sane." He tugged off his boots and stretched atop the bunk. "It keeps my mind off the real reason for this trip."

Bert nodded. Although neither had mentioned it aloud, they had a pact not to speak of the *Wild Card* and their desperate trip upriver to find a way to save her from Lewis Rapper and his auction.

"Now go get yourself some breakfast." Chance waved his friend from the cabin. "We should be pulling into St. Louis by noon. I want to get a few hours sleep before then."

Bert nodded and stepped from the room, leaving Chance alone with the ghost that had haunted him every mile up the Mississippi—the specter of a riverboat he had once owned.

"No, sir." The hotel clerk shook his head. "That's the only wire that arrived for you, Mr. Sharpe."

Chance slipped the unread telegram from Philip Duwayne into his breast pocket. "Would you please double-check? There was supposed to be another message waiting for me here in St. Louis."

The clerk nodded and gave the gambler a polite, the-guest-is-always-right smile and once more checked the mail cubbyhole designated for Chance's room. He then rummaged through a bundle of mail just delivered before turning back again. "I'm sorry, sir, but there's nothing else."

"Thank you." Chance did his best to keep the disappointment from his voice as he motioned for Bert Rooker to follow him up the stairs to a room on the second floor.

Once inside, the riverboat captain looked at his friend. "Things aren't goin' right, are they?"

Chance dropped heavily into an overstuffed chair and drew a deep breath. "I should have heard from Shakey by now."

"Care to tell just who this Shakey is?" Bert arched a thick eyebrow.

"Shakey Haygood," he answered absentmindedly as though he barely heard the question. His thoughts were miles away on the *Wild Card*. All his hopes for regaining ownership of his riverboat rode on his old friend.

"Shakey Haygood—that tells me a hell of a lot, Chance." Bert stared at the gambler. When his friend didn't reply, he asked, "What about the telegram from Philip? What does it say?"

"Huh?" Chance glanced up.

"Philip's wire. Aren't you going to read it?"

Chance slipped the half-forgotten telegram from his coat and unfolded it, and read aloud, "William Forrest is now a legal concern. Have secured the Blasingame plantation for a home office as directed. Rapper has met William's sister and is enchanted." He passed the yellow sheet of paper to Bert. "Philip signed it."

The captain's dark eyes scanned the message. "It looks like the crew back in New Orleans is proceeding right on schedule."

"Wish I could say the same of our progress." He pushed from the chair and walked to a window. Although he stared at the street below, he saw nothing. His thoughts refused to leave his old friend and the man's lack of a reply to his inquiry.

"Well, what do we do now?" Bert placed the telegram on a table.

"Nothing."

"Nothing? You trying to say, there ain't nothing we're going to do?"

"There's nothing we can do, except send another telegram," Chance said. "And wait."

Bert grunted. "Well, there's something I can do, by damn. At least I can unpack my bag!"

Frustrated, the captain grabbed his suitcase and tossed it atop the bed. Before his hands found the buckles to the restraining straps, a knock came from the door. Chance answered it: the hotel clerk stood outside.

"I must apologize about a mistake that's been made,

Mr. Sharpe. Our manager received a wire for you a week ago and placed it in his desk to ensure it didn't get lost." The clerk handed the gambler a telegram.

While the man continued to apologize, Chance opened the message and read: *I have the items you're looking for—S. Haygood.*

Grinning, Chance pivoted to face Bert. "Don't unpack. Soon as I answer this, we're heading up the Ohio for Louisville, Kentucky!"

EIGHT

The steam whistle howled. Long and loud, it screamed out a greeting to the city of Louisville. Again, the near-deafening yowl of steam shattered the late morning. Three times! Five!

In a claustrophobic stateroom that measured ten feet by ten feet, Chance closed a single suitcase and tightly buckled the two restraining straps. He glanced to Captain Bert Rooker, who was busy with a bag of his own. "Ready?"

"In a moment!" Bert grunted and half growled at his suitcase while he wrestled with one of the straps. After several strained tugs, he managed to secure the buckle. "Damned thing's too fancy! Should've brought a sea-man's bag. Drawstring's a damned sight easier to use than this contraption."

Chance smiled at his friend's frustration. As many times as the man traveled the Mississippi and Missouri, it had always been as a member of a boat's crew. The captain was definitely having trouble adjusting to his new role of passenger.

"You feel her jerkin' and arollin' last night? Boat felt like we were in a hurricane!" Bert turned to his companion with suitcase in hand and a disgruntled expression darkening his face. "Must've been a drunkard between the sticks. Surprised we didn't run aground."

"No need to worry now. For the next few days we'll have solid ground beneath our feet."

"It ain't land I'm awantin'." Bert stepped to the stateroom's door and opened it. "It's the deck of my own boat. I've done more riding on another man's steamer than I like."

"That's why we're here." Chance stepped into the main cabin. The stern-wheeler they rode, the *Ohio Runner,* was an old vessel; the passengers' staterooms had but one door, which opened onto the boat's main saloon. "If luck's on our shoulders, all we'll have to do is make one more trip downriver before the *Wild Card*'s ours again."

"It'll be a hell of a long ride." Bert's expression and glum mood remained unchanged by the prospect.

Chance didn't answer as he joined the other passengers who exited the staterooms lining each side of the narrow main saloon and moved toward the double doors at the ends of the long room. He did sympathize with his friend. The journey aboard the *Ohio Runner* had been days of long monotony for him. The boat's captain was a Quaker who would have rather wrestled with the devil himself than allow a poker game aboard his vessel.

Outside, Chance and Bert pressed close to the guard walk's rail, allowing the other passengers to bustle past on their way to the stairways leading to the main deck. Bert grunted again as he stared below to watch roustabouts toss lines to men waiting on the wharf.

"If the same pilot's at the wheel as last night, we're damned lucky he didn't ram us head-on into the dock," Bert said. "A paddlewheeler's a lady who needs a gentle touch to coax her along the currents. Not some oaf jerking her about on the water."

Chance lit a saber to hide his amusement. One glance at Bert's muscular arms provided the truth of the matter. Working a riverboat's wheel for hours upon hours stretched a man to the limit of his endurance and stamina. That "gentle touch" Bert spoke of required arms and a back of steel.

A voice hailed the gambler from below: "Chance! Chance! Here!"

Chance's cool blue eyes surveyed the small sea of faces that stared up at the docking steamer from the wharf. On his second pass he sighted the voice's owner.

"Shakey!" He returned his old friend's wave.

"Which one?" Bert scanned the crowd.

"There." He pointed hastily, then lifted his suitcase from the guard way and stepped toward the steps.

"I don't see—" Bert suddenly noticed he had been left behind. Grabbing his own bag, he half trotted after his friend. "You sure you saw this man we've come to meet?"

"He's here," Chance assured the captain as they took their place behind the other passengers waiting for the gangplank to lower.

Like an ancient drawbridge, the plank eventually did drop. One by one, the passengers, with luggage weighing them down, scurried onto the wharf. Well-wishing relatives moved forward to greet them with hugs, kisses, and tears.

"Chance! Chance Sharpe!" A man standing two inches over five feet pushed through the crowd.

"Damn your eyes, Chance!"

"That's your friend?" Bert stared in disbelief as the short man rushed forward with his right hand extended and a broad grin on his freckled face. "He's the one that's going to help us?"

"Shakey!" Chance accepted the proffered hand and returned the knuckle-cracking grip that tightened like a vise about his fingers. "You look none the worse for the wear, Shakey."

The man chuckled. "Couldn't make weight today if I

tried. Carrie Ann's too good a cook. I eat too well! Can't say the years have done you any harm. You look as fit as a city dog, Chance."

He glanced at all the open-armed greetings around them, then winked at the gambler. "To tell you the truth, I'm so damned glad to see you again that I'd be tempted to give you a hug and kiss, if you weren't as ugly as you've always been."

Bert cleared his throat.

Taking the cue, the gambler turned to the captain. "Bert, I'd like you to meet the finest jockey in Kentucky—Samuel Haygood."

"Shakey," Haygood corrected as he proffered a hand to the riverboat captain. "Nobody calls me Samuel. And forget that jockey business. I haven't ridden since before the war. Since I got married, I've gotten too fat."

"Bert Rooker." The captain winced when Shakey Haygood's hand closed around his.

Chance smiled. The smallness of that hand was deceptive. Years of manhandling high-strung thoroughbreds had given Shakey the strength of a man twice his height.

"This is no place for old friends to lie about the past. There's a restaurant just down the street. I've got a table reserved for us. Thought you might like to get some real food under your belt after eating the slop they serve on riverboats."

The gambler didn't argue. "Lead on."

"Beer?" Shakey Haygood arched an eyebrow and shook his head at Bert's order. "This is Kentucky, my friend. Bourbon's the drink here. Beer's all right for a chaser, but not the main liquid to wet a man's throat."

Bert grinned and nodded, then looked up at the

waiter. "All right, bring me a shot of bourbon with a beer chaser."

"That's better. Have to protect our state industries, especially in rough times like these." Shakey combed his fingers through a full head of cottony blond hair as he glanced across the table at Chance. "It *is* good to see you again. To be honest, I didn't know if you were dead or alive, what with the war taking so many. Did you get called up?"

"Volunteered." The gambler sipped at the mint julip the waiter placed before him. He briefly recounted his military service that led to his rank of captain. "Did a year in Kansas fighting Comanches and Kiowas after the war."

"I took a Yankee lead ball in the left calf early on." Shakey pursed his lips. "Bad enough that they sent me home. I healed up quick, and when no one came to get me again, I decided just to stay."

"Made a hell of a lot more sense than going back," Chance replied. "I think you mentioned something earlier about getting married."

The former jockey beamed from ear to ear. "Carrie Ann Whittier, remember her?"

"That skinny little girl in pigtails that used to chase after you back home?" Chance grinned in surprise.

"That's her, only she grew up in all the right places. We've got two sons and a daughter now."

"Home?" Bert looked at the two men.

"North of here a piece." Shakey answered. "Chance's daddy and mine used to operate a still together back in the woods."

Chance grinned and tilted his head toward his old friend. "He picked up the name 'Shakey' the first time he climbed into a saddle."

"It was my pa," Shakey explained. "He decided that I was too short to be much use for anything else so he took to mind that I was going to be a jockey. Trouble was I'd never sat on a horse before in my life. I was so scared that I was shaking like a leaf. Horse didn't even have to buck. First step it took, I fell off."

"Shakey's old man was fit to be tied," Chance laughed. "Never saw him so angry. Cut a switch from a willow and went after Shakey until he climbed back into the saddle."

"That day I would have killed the old codger if I could have. But I guess he did right by me in the long run. After a couple of spills, I found out I could ride. Horses have been my business ever since."

"Horses?" Bert's eyes widened. His head jerked around to Chance. "You ain't thinking what I'm thinking you're thinking, are you?"

"Depends on what you're thinking."

"That you're about to buy a horse to go up against Rapper's colt," Bert replied.

"Close, but off a bit." Chance took another sip of his drink.

"I'm a little confused, too," Shakey said. "Poker was always your game, Chance. How come you're suddenly interested in horses?"

"It's a long story." The gambler shifted in his chair to allow the waiter to place a platter of steak and potatoes before him. "Sure you wouldn't rather wait until after we've eaten to hear it?"

"We can eat and talk." Shakey sliced into his own beefsteak and popped a juicy bite into his mouth.

"Talk" Bert agreed. "I've been waiting long enough to hear what you've got planned."

As they ate, Chance detailed all that had happened to himself and the *Wild Card*. Steak and potatoes had been replaced by hot pieces of apple pie when he finally said, "Which is why we're here, hoping you can provide the horseflesh needed to win back my river-boat."

"It's crazy," Bert mumbled after hearing the gambler's plan. "It's also shady, Chance."

"No, it's outright cheating," he answered the captain without a trace of shame in his voice. "But I'll do no more to Rapper than he did to me."

"Can't even call it cheating." Shakey's head moved slowly from side to side, then he grinned. "It's just a matter of horse trading."

"Still—" Bert began.

"It'll get the *Wild Card* back," Chance said. "Philip Duwayne will make certain that everything is sewn up nice and tight and legal. All we'll be doing is turning the tables on Rapper."

"I'd prefer to get my hands around the bastard's scrawny neck." Bert reached out and slowly closed his hands into fists as though imagining the feel of the attorney's flesh beneath his fingers.

Chance's own right hand slipped into his coat pocket and pulled out an envelope that he pushed across the table to Shakey. "As I said in my telegram—three thousand dollars in advance. There'll be another five thousand once the job's done, and an additional five thousand bonus if we pull this off. Can you do it for me, Shakey?"

"Thirteen thousand dollars in all. That's a lot of money." The small man's pale blue eyes focused on the envelope, but his hands remained on the table. "And all I have to do is ship two horses to Louisiana and race them in two races. You don't even want to buy my horses?"

"The horses remain yours. Just get them downriver still healthy and sound. And have them ready to race when I say."

Shakey's blond head dubiously moved from side to

side, but he reached out and took the envelope. "It's your money. I guess you know what you're doing."

"Let's hope I do," Chance replied.

"Pray you do," Bert added, uncertainty masking his face.

"I reckon you'd like to see what you're getting for your money," Shakey said. "My farm's about sixty miles from here. If you're ready, we might as well get going. We've got a good day and a half ride ahead of us."

"Then let's get started," Chance answered, pushing away from the table.

Together the three men left the restaurant and climbed into the carriage Shakey had tied and waiting outside. Chance's heart tripled its pace when his friend brought a bay mare to life with a pop of a whip and the carriage jerked forward.

I'm committed, he thought with a soft sigh escaping his lips. Whether he traveled the course of a wild man or journeyed toward eventual success, only time would tell.

NINE

A rooster crowed rudely outside the bedroom window.

With a mumbled curse, Chance rolled to his back. The errant fowl produced another grating cry. The gambler groaned, blinked bleary eyes, and glanced to the window.

Through the heavy limbs of an oak tree that stood beyond the pane of glass, he could barely discern a murky gray sky of morning. *What time is it anyway?*

The rooster crowed once more as though answering the unspoken question.

Damned bird's up too early. It's not dawn yet. Chance threw an arm over his face to blot out the diffused light that entered through the window. It was hours before he usually rose to greet a new day.

The enticing aromas of steaming coffee, baking biscuits, and sizzling bacon wafted in the air, tantalizing his nostrils. The gambler's mouth watered; his stomach rumbled in protest.

Outside, the rooster squawked persistently.

"Enough," he conceded.

Between the overly vocal bird and the beckoning smells, he couldn't win. No matter how early the hour he would never return to sleep until he sated his suddenly ravenous hunger—or strangled the noisy rooster.

Tossing back the bed covers, the gambler swung his long legs over the side of the bed and stood. After a stretching yawn, he quickly washed the sleep from his

75

face in a basin that sat atop a small table beside the bed. For a moment he tested the stubble covering his cheeks and chin.

He decided to ignore it. No man who was half-asleep should ever allow a razor close to his throat! Even if it was in his own hand!

Tugging on a pair of tan breeches and a white shirt he pulled from his suitcase, he dug out a pair of clean socks and managed to find his black boots nearly hidden beneath the bed, where he had kicked them last night before collapsing atop the feather mattress.

Still blinking to remove the last traces of sleep cotton from his eyes, he left the bedroom and wandered down a narrow hallway to an equally narrow flight of stairs that led to the house's first floor. There he followed the beckoning aromas to the back of the house where he found Bert Rooker already seated at a kitchen table.

"Chance?" This from Carrie Ann Haygood, Shakey's wife, who pulled a pan of biscuits from the stove and placed them on the table. "Captain Rooker here said it would be midday before you woke. Can I get you a cup of coffee?"

Chance nodded and took a chair beside Rooker. "Does anyone happen to know what time it is?"

"About five," Carrie Anne answered cheerfully as she poured the gambler's coffee. "Shakey's already had his breakfast and gone to the barn. Children won't be up until seven or so."

"Already at the barn?" Chance looked at the handsome young woman, attempting to picture her as the skinny little runt in pigtails that he once had known.

He couldn't. Shakey had been right. Carrie Ann had grown up in all the right places. He could well imagine the heads she had turned before she had married the former jockey. Shakey was a lucky man—a damned lucky man.

"We're up by four around here. This isn't the city. It's a farm." Carrie Ann placed a platter heaped with thick-cut bacon on the table, then pushed a jar of strawberry jam toward the men. "Best eat up. It's a long time until lunch."

"Mind if I just make myself a couple of bacon-and-biscuit sandwiches? I'd like to join Shakey." Chance couldn't imagine the man already at work. They hadn't arrived at the farm until midnight—mere hours ago.

"Take the coffee with you, as long as you bring the cup back," Carrie Ann replied. "Remind Shakey to do the same. He's always forgetting his down at the barn. About once a week I have to send one of the children to collect them. If I didn't, I wouldn't have one left in the house."

Using a knife to open three of the still-steaming biscuits, Chance spread a thick layer of jam in each, then settled a crisp piece of bacon atop the sweet, red bed. Biscuits balanced in one hand and coffee cup in the other, he rose.

Carrie Ann opened the kitchen's door and pointed. "Barn's straight to the east. Can't miss it."

"Bert, you coming?" he paused at the threshold to glance back at his friend.

"Later." The captain smiled and waved his hands toward the food piled before him. "You might be foolish enough to leave all this. I'm not."

Chance grinned, turned, and stepped across a wooden porch to a path that led toward the barn. His gaze took in the beauty of the land that surrounded him.

The Haygood home was a sturdy two-story brick structure. A grove of ancient, twisted oaks grew about the white-trimmed home. Beyond the trees were gently rolling pastures of deep green Kentucky bluegrass. Whitewashed fences stood in sharp contrast to the lush

vegetation. Here and there mares with young colts
stood grazing in the ankle-deep fields.

For a moment, Chance felt a haunting tug at his
heart. This was Kentucky, his childhood home. He
could not deny the effect the land had on him. Memories of family and friends crowded into his head. He
savored each, then gently placed them in their correct
niche. Once Kentucky had been his home, no longer.
As a boy of thirteen he had run away from his father's
farm to answer the call of the river. For most of his life
the Mississippi had been his home; he had no regrets.

Nor did he allow the beauty of these pastures to blind
him to the truth. It took work—hard work—to build
the farm his friend had managed here. Nor did the work
ever stop. Horses were a twenty-four-hour-a-day,
seven-days-a-week job, especially those bred for the
sport of kings.

"Chance!" Shakey called to him.

Chance glanced up to find his friend waving from the
open doors of a barn that lay directly ahead. "Shakey."

"Didn't figure to see you until noon or so," Shakey
said as the gambler approached. "Captain Rooker said
you were a late sleeper."

"Normally I am. But I wanted to see the 'items' you
mentioned in your wire."

"Then you're just in time." The former jockey motioned his friend toward the left. "I was just walking
down to watch one of the colts work."

Placing his empty coffee cup on the ground near the
front of the barn, Chance hastened after Shakey, whose
brisk steps carried him toward an open field a quarter
mile from the barn. "These colts are three-year-olds,
aren't they?"

Shakey nodded. "That's what you asked for, wasn't
it? Both have the same sire, but are out of different
dams. They've got their pappy's lines and conforma-

tion, but they get their distance from their mamas. It's uncanny . . . Hell, no need me talking about it. I'll let you judge for yourself."

Chance wasn't too certain about that. His expertise was the gaming tables. He was depending on Shakey to provide the horseflesh and knowledge needed to beat Lewis Rapper's colt. However, he kept quiet and followed his friend to the edge of the open field.

"The tall posts are quarter-mile markers. The smaller ones each mark an eighth of a mile." Shakey pointed to a series of posts sunk at the center of the field. "The course around the posts is a half mile."

The gambler studied the roughly oval shape the posts described. Shakey and he stood beside the midpoint of the nearest long, flat stretch. The turn to his right was wide and sweeping. To the left he opposite turn looked pinched and slightly angular.

"Are we going to be racing on a straightaway, cross-country, or marked course?" Shakey glanced at Chance.

The gambler shook his head. "I don't know. Does it matter?"

"It might." Shakey bit at his lower lip. "When we get downriver, I'll want to work my horses over the course a few times before they race. The more familiar the colts are with the land, the better they'll run. The jock needs to know the course, too."

"I think that should be easy enough to arrange."

Shakey leaned forward, plucked a blade of grass, and placed it in the corner of his mouth. For long, silent moments, he busied the grass with tongue and teeth before spitting it out.

"You know, Chance, I can't guarantee anything." Worry lined the former jockey's face. He rubbed a hand through his blond hair. "I'm not a miracle worker. These colts of mine are good, damned good, but they don't call it a horse race for nothing. On any given day a horse can be beaten, no matter how good he is."

"I understand that. It's a risk I'm willing to take," the gambler replied. "However, risks can be lessened by honing an edge as sharp as possible. That's why I'm here. There's no better man with horses than you."

"There's always a better man and a better horse, Chance," Shakey answered. "I just wanted to make certain that you realize the situation. You've got a hell of a lot riding on this. You could lose it all."

"I've already lost it." Bitterness seeped into the gambler's voice. "What you and your colts are going to give me is a way to win it back."

Shakey nodded. "Just as sure as you know what you're getting into."

"I know," the gambler answered. "I know."

Turning, Shakey waved back to the barn. A groom standing by the open door returned the signal and darted inside the structure. A few moments later a black colt in saddle and bridle with an exercise boy on his back stepped from the barn and moved toward the field.

Chance studied the sleek animal in the growing golden light of predawn. The three-year-old stood fifteen hands, if he stood an inch. His muscular neck bowed and strained against the bit in his mouth and the strong hold his rider held on him. The gambler could feel the power in the colt's broad chest and the prancing of his long legs. The horse wanted to run!

"Pull him up here for a moment, Earlie," Shakey ordered the exercise boy. "I want Chance to take a close look at Haygood's Lad."

"Chance Sharpe," the gambler said, introducing himself to the rider when Shakey took the horse's head.

"Pleased to meet you, Mr. Sharpe. The name's Earlie Sutton," the exercise boy answered in a voice as youthful as his unblemished face. "Take your time. You won't find a thing wrong with Haygood's Lad. He's as fit as a fiddle."

Running a palm down the horse's neck, Chance patted the animal's chest before squatting at the three-year-old's left side and easing his hand down Haygood's Lad's left foreleg. He carefully felt all four legs before rising again.

"Knees, shins, and ankles all feel sound. No swelling, no heat," Chance said to his old friend.

Shakey smiled and looked up at the exercise boy. "Lope him around once to loosen him up, Earlie. Then I want you to give him a full workout for a mile."

"A mile?" Puzzlement twinged Earlie's tone.

"A mile," Shakey repeated, then released the horse's head.

Earlie moved onto the course and clucked Haygood's Lad into an easy lope.

"Earlie's my rider," Shakey said as he looked back to the gambler. "He's only fifteen, but he's got more horse sense about him than I've ever had. The best jockey in this part of the state."

"If he's your choice, he's mine," Chance answered, watching the young rider and horse as they moved around the first turn. "Earlie certainly looks like he knows his business."

"He does. So does the colt." Shakey dug a hand into a pants pocket to produce a stopwatch that he passed to his friend. "Here, you time him. Earlie will break the moment he's even with us."

Chance took the timepiece, cleared it, then poised his thumb to start the watch. Around the left turn Haygood's Lad came in a steady lope under Earlie's tight rein. Down the stretch they moved.

The instant horse and rider reached the two men's position, Earlie lessened his hold, tapped his heels to the colt's side, and shouted. Haygood's Lad broke into a full run. Chance's thumb fell; the stopwatch began counting the seconds.

"Twenty-four," the gambler called out in amazement as the horse reached the quarter pole on the opposite side of the course.

Head stretched before him and ears pinned back, Haygood's Lad never broke his stride as he reached and rounded the pinched turn. Dirt and grass flew from his hooves as he shot down the stretch past the two men who watched.

Chance's amazement remained as he announced the time for the half mile: "Forty-nine."

Unflagging, the three-year-old ran. Without a whip, Earlie's hands moved up and down on the horse's neck, urging him onward.

"One fifteen," Chance read as colt and rider reached the three-quarter pole.

At that instant Haygood's Lad ran head-on into an invisible brick wall. That three-quarters of a mile burst of speed had played out. Run as he did, the colt might as well have been galloping.

"No need to look at the watch anymore," Shakey said to his friend. "This colt's a sprinter. Ain't much around that can match him at three-quarters of a mile After that a plow horse could take him."

"He's the perfect bait," Chance answered, making no attempt to hide his pleasure with Shakey's first colt. "If your second horse performs as well as Haygood's Lad, then Lewis Rapper is as good as mine."

"Earlie," Shakey called to the young rider as he reined a worn-out Haygood's Lad from the course. "Chance wants to take a look at Kentucky Rambler next. Have Del put the tack on him while Ned cools out this colt."

Earlie nodded and maneuvered Haygood's Lad back toward the barn. For seconds Chance watched the horse with a pleased grin on his face. Shakey had understood exactly what he wanted from this colt. His pulse doubled in anticipation of Kentucky Rambler's performance.

"Chance, you ever hear from your brothers?" Shakey abruptly asked from out of the blue.

The gambler turned to the former jockey. "Saw Matt while the army had me in Kansas. He's got a farm, wife, and three kids. Seemed to be doing good."

"And Wyatt?" Shakey asked.

"Last time either Matt or I heard from him was at Pa's funeral." Chance recalled that rainy day in '49 before gold fever had drawn him to California. His youngest brother had been distraught over their father's death. "He said something about heading west. Matt received one letter from him postmarked Oregon. That was right before the war broke out. Haven't heard a word from him since."

Shakey sucked at his teeth, but said nothing more. Nor did Chance. What could be said? After his parents' deaths, he and his brothers had gone their separate ways. The call of a young nation was too strong to hold them to a plot of land in Kentucky.

"Here's the second colt." Shakey pointed to the barn.

The gambler's jaw sagged as he stared at the second animal Earlie rode toward the training course. Kentucky Rambler might have been the twin to Haygood's Lad; the two horses appeared identical!

"Same sire, different dams," Shakey repeated, obviously amused by the amazement on his friend's face. "Unless you've raised them the way I have, it's damned hard to tell one colt from the other."

"Perfect." Chance felt the colt's legs when Earlie

stopped beside him. Again he found no trace of heat or
swelling.

"Give him the same ride you gave Haygood's Lad,"
Shakey said, sending the young jockey onto the course.

Clearing the stopwatch, Chance watched the three-
year-old colt slowly lope around the lopsided oval. He
started the timepiece the instant Earlie urged the horse
into a run.

"Twenty-five and change," Chance called out as
Kentucky Rambler reached the quarter pole. Slower
than the first colt, he realized, but that was to be expected. Kentucky Rambler was a distance runner.

Nor was he bothered by the fifty-one-second time at
the half mile. His eyebrows did arch when the colt had
turned only a minute and twenty at the three-quarter
pole, but he prepared himself for a spectacular dash
that last quarter of a mile.

It didn't come. Kentucky Rambler's easy stride
never increased. The horse had barely worked up a
lather on his chest when he crossed the mile marker
with a time of one minute and fifty seconds.

"Shakey?" Chance turned to the former jockey at his
side with uncertainty. "This is the horse you wanted me
to see?"

Shakey laughed. "Kentucky Rambler is the right
horse. Don't worry, Chance, I'm not leading you down
the garden path. I just wanted you to see him like this
first. Tomorrow, we'll let him rest. Then two days from
now, I'll show you what he's really made of."

As Earlie reined the horse from the course, Shakey
stepped beside the horse and began walking back to the
barn.

Chance stared at his friend, still unable to compre-
hend what Shakey had wanted him to see in the horse.
Had the man completely lost his mind? A horse that

was only ten seconds off two minutes for a mile run would never beat Lewis Rapper's colt.

"Damn," Chance muttered with the realization that his scheme for winning back the *Wild Card* was crumbling under him.

TEN

Two mornings after Kentucky Rambler's disappointing workout, a skeptical Chance once more walked with his friend Shakey Haygood to the training field. Behind them trailed Captain Bert Rooker, looking lost so far from the Mississippi River and her currents.

Reaching the side of the course, Shakey passed the gambler the stopwatch once again. He then waved back to the barn.

"Shakey, are you certain this is necessary?" he asked unable to conceal his doubt. "I've seen the colt once. I—"

The former jockey shook his head, waved his hands, and laughed. "You've only seen one side of Kentucky Rambler. I guarantee what I'm going to show you today will change your mind. This *is* the second colt you want, only you don't know it yet."

Shakey turned to Bert. "What did you say Rapper's colt was clocked at for a mile?"

"A minute and forty-two seconds," the captain answered. "That's a mite faster than a minute fifty."

Shakey laughed again as he looked back to the barn. Two horses and riders stepped from the structure side by side. Sharpe recognized the black form of Kentucky Rambler, but had never seen the bay beside him.

"What's this?" The gambler arched an eyebrow in question.

"This is what the colt's all about," Shakey assured

his two companions. "The bay's a five-year-old gelding named No Joke. Last year he won nineteen out of twenty starts all at distances of a mile or more. This year he's had ten straight wins. His time for the mile is usually around one forty-two."

"The same as Rapper's colt," Bert said.

Too bad the bay isn't black, Chance thought. *Then maybe we'd stand a chance against Rapper.*

"The rider on No Joke is Ned Kieper," Shakey continued. "Ned rides for me when Earlie has other mounts. He can handle a horse well."

Chance didn't speak, just stared at the two horses as they drew to a halt before the jockey-turned-trainer. The amused glint remained in Shakey's eyes as though he had something up his sleeve. Chance wasn't impressed; he had seen the three-year-old work two days earlier.

"Earlie, Ned, line 'em up. You're going to break from a standing start and take 'em a mile," Shakey ordered the two jockeys. "I want you to ride this just like it was a race with heavy money riding on your horses' noses. Understand?"

Both the riders nodded and turned their mounts toward the training course.

"Start at my signal," Shakey called after them, then turned to his two companions. "If you'd like to make this interesting, I'll take Kentucky Rambler and give you five to one odds."

"I'll take some of that," Bert answered as he pulled ten dollars from a pocket.

"You, Chance?" Shakey eyed his friend. "Willing to wager a few dollars?"

"I'll keep my money in my wallet," Chance answered. Maybe Shakey *was* hiding something; maybe the colt had more than he had displayed the other morning.

"My daddy used to say that it made no never-mind that a man knew a fly didn't chew tobacco," Shakey said. "You just saved yourself a wet face, Chance."

"Fly chewin' tobacco? What's he mean?" Bert looked at the gambler.

"It's something Shakey's pa used to tell us when we were boys," Chance replied with a smile. "It doesn't matter that a man knows a fly doesn't chew tobacco, because one day someone is going to bet you that a fly *can* chew tobacco. As soon as you place your money on the table, the man who offered the bet is going to pull a plug from a pocket and a fly from another. That fly is going to alight on the tobacco, take a big chaw, then fly right up and spit in your face!"

"It's another way of saying don't buy a pig in a poke." Shakey chuckled as he glanced to the training course.

Earlie and Ned had their mounts lined up and ready. The two horses pranced impatiently as though aware of the race that lay ahead of them.

Shakey lifted his right arm, then let it fall. Sharpe clicked the stopwatch to life.

The five-year-old and three-year-old broke neck and neck. They remained that way through the stretch as they went into the first turn. No Joke had the younger colt by a nose when they came out of the turn.

"Twenty-four," Chance announced as No Joke reached the quarter-mile post half a length ahead of Kentucky Rambler.

That lead had increased to a full length by the time the older, more experienced horse passed the half-mile marker in forty-nine seconds.

"Tobacco-chewin' flies, my ass," Bert crowed. "Looks like I've made myself an easy fifty dollars."

Chance's mouth opened to agree with the captain. He held his tongue and swallowed hard.

Kentucky Rambler, beneath Earlie's urging hands, came to life. Like a man getting a second wind, the three-year-old lunged forward, its long legs stretching out to cover the ground beneath it. The colt had regained half the lost length by the time No Joke shot past the three-quarters pole in a minute and sixteen seconds.

Chance doubled-checked the time. The speed was only a second off Haygood's Lad's time. And that colt was a sprinter!

"That's it, Earlie. Bring him on," Shakey yelled, shouting encouragement to the jockey. "Bring him on!"

The young rider did exactly that. With only a furlong separating the two horses from the mile post, the jockeys battled it out on mounts running nose to nose.

"Right now!" Shakey shouted, pointing to Kentucky Rambler. "Watch him make his move!"

The black colt bounded forward. Neck held straight out and ears pinned back, he leaped forward. In two strides he had nosed ahead of the more experienced horse. By the time he crossed the finish, he was half a length ahead of No Joke.

Sharpe clicked the stopwatch and stared in disbelief at the face.

"Well?" Shakey asked. "Just under one forty-two?"

"One forty-one and fifty-eight," the gambler muttered, still uncertain whether to believe his own eyes.

"I think you owe me ten dollars." The jockey-turned-trainer took the money from Bert's hand and stuffed it into his own pocket. "Want a handkerchief to wipe the tobacco juice out of your eyes?"

"I think I need one." Bert's amazed gaze remained on the two horses as they pulled up and trotted back around the course.

As happy as a child on Christmas morning, Shakey

looked back at the gambler. "Well, Chance, what do you think of Kentucky Rambler now?"

"That's not the same horse I saw two days ago." He studied the stopwatch again: the time remained the same.

"Same horse, same jock, same course," Shakey assured him. "Only thing different was the circumstances. The colt was running against another horse. That's the secret—Kentucky Rambler needs to go up against another horse."

Chance glanced at his old friend. A glimmering of Shakey's meaning began to penetrate his brain.

"You wouldn't believe how disappointed I was in the colt the first few times I worked him," Shakey said. "It wasn't until I brought him out with another horse that I realized just what I had. He won't let another horse beat him! He's got to have a challenge before he'll run."

"Won't let another horse beat him?" Chance stared at the trainer.

"That's the way of it. He puts out just enough to win. Put him up against a slower horse, and he'll run a slow race, but he'll win," Shakey said. "Give him a horse with speed, and he'll show you a heart as big as this country—and he'll win!"

"Heart," Chance repeated. A smile slowly spread across his face to replace a dumbfounded expression. "The colt needs competition!"

Shakey laughed and reached up to slap his friend on the shoulder. "You've finally got it. He'll run all day and night as long as another horse is challenging him. I've matched him up to a mile and a half. He hasn't been beaten in ten starts."

"What did he turn in at that distance?" Chance's interest was definitely piqued.

"Two minutes and fifty seconds," Shakey replied,

obviously proud of the time. "And he didn't even look winded."

From the corner of his eye, the gambler watched Bert step forward to get a closer look at the three-year-old colt as Earlie reined him past their position on a route back to the barn. The riverboat captain made no attempt to hide his admiration for the animal.

"Think Kentucky Rambler will suit the bill?" Shakey asked when he started after the two horses.

"I think that I came to the right man," Chance answered, feeling a twinge of guilt for doubting his old friend's judgment when it came to horseflesh. "Both colts are exactly what I'm looking for."

Exhilaration coursed through the gambler as he walked at the trainer's side back to the barn. For the first time since Rapper had gained the title to the *Wild Card* he saw a light of hope.

A blazing beacon, he mentally corrected himself. If Philip Duwayne and Katie MacArt built a strong foundation back in New Orleans, Shakey had just given him the hand needed to beat Rapper at his own game.

Of course, there was still a hell of a lot that had to be done, and all the pieces had to neatly fall into place, but now he had an even chance of regaining his riverboat. A man couldn't argue with odds like that.

"Ned, Earlie, after the horses are washed down, I want them cooled out nice and slow. At least an hour, and be careful how you water them. No more than three gulps at a time," Shakey called out as he entered the barn.

Chance and Bert followed him into the long brick structure. Ten stalls lined each side of the stable, separated by a shedrow twenty feet in width. A second pair of double doors were open at the opposite end of the barn. A quarter of mile beyond, the framework of another barn was under construction.

"It's in line with this one," Shakey said, noticing the gambler's gaze. "That way I can keep an eye on what's going on in the other no matter which barn I'm in."

"These horses get better care than some men I know," Bert said, watching as both Kentucky Rambler and No Joke were bathed in hot soapy water, rinsed, scraped dry, and then covered in a blanket before being led outside, where they would be walked until they had cooled from their race.

"This isn't the half of it," Shakey answered. "Sometimes I think I give them better treatment than I give myself."

He gave the captain a thumbnail sketch of how the horses would be currycombed and brushed when they were returned to their stalls. Grooms would then massage their legs with a brace.

"That's not mentioning their diet—oats, bran, carrots, hay, and alfalfa," Shakey said. "There's a lot of time and money invested in these horses. They're no good to anyone unless they're fit to run."

Bert scratched at his thick muttonchop sideburns and shook his head. "Sounds like as much work as it takes to keep a paddlewheeler afloat."

"Pretty near, I'd say," the trainer replied. "Pretty near."

"Boss, you got a minute?" A man's voice sounded behind the three.

A cold shiver shut up Chance's spine when he turned to locate the voice's owner. A square-headed man with short-cropped brown hair stood in the doorway of a stall five feet away.

The man's brown eyes glanced at the gambler, showing no sign of recognition. Chance could not say the same thing. He had seen the man before. Where?

"This filly's got a little heat in her right ankle," the man continued. "Want to take a look at it?"

Shakey nodded and disappeared into the stall. Casually, Chance drifted after him. While the former jockey's knowledgeable hands tested the questionable ankle, the gambler studied the groom who watched on.

Chance estimated the barrel-chested man's height as equal to his own six feet. However, the groom's weight was again half that of the gambler's. He was built square and solid with arms like tree trunks and hands the size of hams.

Where? Chance repeated the question to himself. He was certain he knew the man, but couldn't place him. Nor could he explain the feeling of dread that the groom awoke at the pit of his stomach. *Where?*

"There is a little heat," Shakey said as he stood and walked from the stall. "Make sure she's in bandages today, Del, and I'll take another look tomorrow."

The trainer glanced back at Chance and Bert. "Want another look at Haygood's Lad?"

Chance nodded yes and moved to the colt's stall at his friend's side. "Del? Is that what you called that groom?"

"Del. Del Taggart," Shakey answered while he opened the stall's door. "Why?"

"I swear that I've met him before. But the name doesn't ring any bells."

"He's the best man I've got on the farm." Shakey took the colt by the halter and led him out of the stall. "In fact, I've just made him my foreman. Came to me right after the war. Knows a hell of a lot about horses."

Chance shook his head. Although he was certain he had met Del Taggart before, he still couldn't remember where or when. "Must be confusing him with someone else."

"Well, Bert, now that you've seen both colts, what do you think?" Shakey waved a hand toward Haygood's Lad.

The captain's eyes shot toward Kentucky Rambler, who was still outside being cooled, then back to the colt Shakey held. "They look like the same horse to me! I can't tell one from the other, and I'm looking at both of them!"

"Exactly!" Chance grinned. "And they'll look like the same colt to Lewis Rapper."

"Then I reckon you've made your decision?" Shakey glanced at Chance. "These colts are what you're looking for?"

"I don't think we could find any better," the gambler replied.

Shakey returned Haygood's Lad to the stall and closed the door. "If you're satisfied with the colts, then I guess the only thing I have to ask is, when do you want to start downriver with them?"

"As soon as possible," Chance replied. Each passing day brought them twenty-four hours closer to Rapper's scheduled auction.

"How about we get started tomorrow?" Shakey lifted an expectant eyebrow.

"Sounds good to me."

"Good. I'll send Del ahead of us to Louisville today. He'll book passage for us on a steamer heading south. He'll also arrange whatever is needed to handle the colts while aboard," the trainer answered. "Earlie and the three of us will leave with the colts tomorrow as soon as the morning's work is done. Should be in Louisville three days from now."

Chance quickly calculated the time needed to reach Baton Rouge. Three and a half weeks would remain before Rapper's auction. It would be a tight squeeze, but time enough to bait and spring the trap.

ELEVEN

Shakey Haygood tugged on the reins, halting the chestnut mare he rode. His head turned from side to side, then he pointed to the left.

"That stand of trees looks like as good a spot as any for a rest." He turned to Chance. "Need to give the horses a rest and let them graze a bit."

"Wouldn't hurt to put some grub in our own bellies," Bert added. "I'll volunteer to fry some bacon, if someone else will make the coffee. Never could brew coffee. 'Course, if you want me to, I'll give her a try."

Chance spoke up quickly: "I'll handle the coffee." The first night on the road Bert had brewed the coffee —to the regret of everyone. "There's no need to poison all of us."

Bert grunted when Shakey and Earlie chuckled, then reined his bay toward the copse of oaks.

"Still got a few of the biscuits Carrie Ann baked us in my saddlebags," Shakey said. "I'll bring them over as soon as I see to the colts."

The trainer tilted his head toward a stand of knee-high grass to the left of the oaks. "Let's stake them out there, Earlie. Then we'll see about finding some water."

While Shakey and the jockey turned their mounts and led the two black colts toward the grass, Chance nudged the sides of the buckskin he rode and moved forward to join Bert beneath the trees. Locating a low, overhanging limb, he dismounted and tied the horse's reins to the branch. After securing the packhorse he led to another branch, he took a smoke-blackened pot and a sack of ground coffee from his saddlebags. The water in his canteen completed the ingredients needed for the promised brew.

Placing all three on the ground beside a pile of dried leaves and small twigs Bert had gathered for kindling, Chance helped his friend locate larger branches for the fire. Five minutes and two matches later, a small blaze crackled to life. He poured a healthy measure of coffee into the pot, filled it with water, and then set the container to one side of the flames.

Bert paused after filling a skillet with strips of bacon. "Am I crazy for thinkin' this just might work, Chance?" His head lifted and he stared at the two grazing colts. "No matter how many times I look at them, I can't tell one from the other."

Chance summoned all the bravado he could muster, refusing to allow his own doubts to creep into his voice. "It will work. Rapper will come to us like a fly drawn to sugar. He won't be able to resist. We'll be playing on his two weaknesses—horses and greed."

Bert nodded silently as he flipped the bacon with the end of a hunting knife. "What if Rapper's colt is like Kentucky Rambler? What if he won't let another horse beat him?"

"That's highly unlikely, Bert. And if his colt is that good, then we're in for one hell of a horse race."

The frown on the captain's face said that the possibility brought him little comfort. "Wonder how Henri and Katie are doing? How well do they have Rapper primed—"

Bert's questions were left unanswered; Shakey and Earlie rode into the trees and dismounted.

"Found a stream just over that rise," Shakey said as

he settled on the ground beside the camp fire. "We'll ride over and water the horses after we've eaten."

"Hmmmm, that coffee smells good." The young jockey held a tin cup ready in his right hand. "How soon before it's ready, Mr. Sharpe?"

"A few more minutes. And it's Forrest, Earlie, William Forrest."

Chance's eyes narrowed as his gaze turned to his other two companions. "All of you have to remember that. Until I've gotten Rapper's signature transferring ownership of the *Wild Card,* I'm William Forrest. One slip of the tongue and our bird will take wing. Understand?"

All three of the men gathered around the fire nodded. Earlie said aloud, "William Forrest. I won't forget again, Mr. Forrest."

Chance smiled and looked at Shakey. "I think you mentioned something about some biscuits?"

"Right here!" The horse trainer held up a knotted flour sack. "All they need is some bacon to go with them."

"And a little coffee," Chance added, lifting the pot and holding it toward the young jockey. "Let's see that cup, Earlie."

A crack, like thunder splitting the sky, rolled from the right. An invisible fist slammed into the pot, jarring it from the gambler's hand. Steaming coffee showered the air to spill onto the ground.

Bert jerked around. "What the—"

"Behind the trees!" Chance's blue eyes homed on the pot. A clean, round hole, the unmistakable signature of a bullet, had opened the container's side. "Move! Get behind the trees!"

The gambler lunged for the protection of the nearest oak bole. A second shot rang out. Hot angry lead buzzed by the gambler's right ear, expending itself in a shower of splinters as it slammed into the tree trunk.

Pressing himself flat behind the oak, Chance unsheathed the .44 Remington holstered on his right hip. Cautiously, he poked his head around the trunk, searching for the unseen gunman or gunmen.

Nothing. He neither saw nor heard a trace of the hidden assailant. He glanced at Bert Rooker, who stood with his back pressed against an oak five feet away.

"Can't make 'em out," the captain answered as he drew a pistol from his belt. "Second shot came too fast to make their position."

Shakey and Earlie, crouched behind a tree together, shrugged and shook their heads.

The glint of sunlight along a rifle barrel flared beside a double-trunked poplar across the road from the oaks. Chance jerked back as a third shot barked. Again lead harmlessly spent itself in the oak's trunk.

"Got him," Bert called to his companion. "One man about a hundred yards from here. He's reloading."

"Cover me!"

The captain answered by taking a swinging stride out from behind the oak. Both arms steadying his weapon, he leveled the revolver at the poplars and squeezed the trigger.

As the first harsh report exploded, Chance darted from the security of the trunk sheltering him. Racing to his mount, he snatched the horse's reins from the overhanging branch and tossed them over the buckskin's head.

The horse shied back from the sudden movement. The gambler ignored the frightened back-stepping and swung into the saddle. Reins in his left hand, pistol cocked and ready in his right, he jerked the buckskin's head around.

"There's only one of 'em. He's mounting!" Bert

shouted above the bark of his third shot. "He's running for it!"

Chance's heels dug into his mount's flanks. Ducking beneath low limbs that could drag him from the saddle, he reined for the road and the stand of trees beyond.

Sunlight splashed over the gunman's green shirt and black trousers as he scrambled atop a bay. Chance's eyes narrowed to slits as he watched the unknown assailant tug the bay's head around and spur the horse westward, but it was too distant to make out the man's features.

The gambler leveled his Remington and squeezed off a round as the horse and rider raced from behind the protection of the poplars: a wasted shot. Man and beast were beyond the range of the .44. His heel slapped against the buckskin's flanks again, urging greater speed.

The instant his mount's hooves hit the open road, the gunman spurred the bay with each long stride of its legs. From side to side he slapped his reins, using the leather as another man might use a whip.

Around a sharp turn in the road, the gambler rode after the unknown rider. As he reined the buckskin around a second turn a half mile from the first, he tugged back, easing the horse to a halt.

The road ahead was empty!

Chance's head jerked from left to right, surveying the heavy wood that pushed to the road's edge on each side. He had no doubt the fleeing man had taken to the trees to escape, but which way?

A touch of his heels and the buckskin moved forward. The gambler's eyes shifted from one side of the road to the other. Fifty feet from where he had halted, he found telltale tracks that veered northward. Pistol ready to meet attack, he moved off the road following them.

Aware that the gunman might lie in ambush behind any of the thick, ancient boles, Chance rode with senses alert for any movement, the slightest sound that might warn him of an attack. There was nothing, only an occasional blue jay that flitted among the gnarled oak limbs.

The trail ended abruptly a mile into the forest. The deep-cut hoofprints led into a swiftly flowing, crystal-clear stream, and then vanished. The creekbed of pebble and stone gave no hint as to which way the gunman had fled.

"Son of a bitch!" Chance cursed, halting the buckskin to allow the horse to lower its head for a well-deserved drink.

Realizing the uselessness of continuing the pursuit, he conceded defeat. The man had planned his escape well. Even if the gambler knew the direction the gunman had taken, the time wasted in tracking him through the wood had given the fleeing man too much of an edge. Chance could never hope to overtake him now.

Pulling his mount's head from the water, he turned the horse around and began retracing his path through the forest.

"Chance!" Shakey's voice hailed him as he neared the road.

Through the trees Chance saw his friends mounted and waiting for him. He waved and urged his horse forward in a trot.

"The bastard got away," he said, recounting all that had occurred.

"Probably should count ourselves lucky," the trainer said with a shake of his head. "Since the war a lot of men have fallen on hard times. Some think it's easier to make a go of it with a gun."

Chance didn't argue as they reined their horses back toward the camp. The possibility that the gunman had intended to rob them couldn't be overlooked. In all likelihood that had been the man's purpose.

The only thing that rubbed at the gambler was why had all three of the man's shots been aimed at him?

"We'll take the horses aboard first," Captain Jack Norwood explained with a tilt of his head toward the *Pearl Brown,* sitting moored at the end of wharf. "My crew's built a pen for your animals near the prow. But I think things will be safer all around if the rest of the cargo is piled around the pen."

Chance glanced at the white stern-wheeler. Crates and sacks of cargo were piled on the pier along her one-hundred-seventy-five-foot length. Roustabouts stood idly by, awaiting a signal to begin the back-bending task of loading.

"Whenever you're ready, we'll get them aboard," Shakey answered the captain.

"No time better than now," Norwood answered.

Shakey nodded and turned to his foreman Del Taggart. "Del, you go first with Kentucky Rambler. He's a bit less spirited than Haywood's Lad. If the other colt sees him cross the gangplank first, things might go easier. Earlie, lead Haygood's Lad right after Del."

The gambler watched the foreman take a hold on Kentucky Rambler's shank just below the horse's halter and start toward the riverboat. Gone was the cold shiver that had coursed along Chance's spine when he had first seen the man, but he still could not shake the sensation that he and Taggart had met before under less than desirable circumstances.

"That's it," Shakey called to his foreman. "Take it nice and easy."

Kentucky Rambler stepped onto the gangplank without hesitation and walked aboard the steamer with no more than a swish of his long black tail. Del led the colt into the waiting pen and held him there.

Such was not the case with Haygood's Lad: the sprinter reached the gangplank and balked. Although the young jockey coaxed and tugged, the horse locked his legs and refused to budge.

"Lead him back, walk him around some, and try again," Shakey suggested.

Earlie did as told—three times. And with each try to board the stern-wheeler, Haygood's Lad displayed a stubborn streak to rival that of a mule. The horse refused to place a hoof on the gangplank.

"Damn!" Shakey hastened beside the colt. "Let me get his feet on the boards."

Reaching down, the horse trainer used the pressure of thumb and forefinger behind the animal's left knee to unlock the leg. He then lifted the horse's hoof and placed in onto the gangplank. Edging to Haygood Lad's opposite side, he repeated the process with the right leg.

Still the colt refused to move an inch, no matter how hard Earlie tugged at his halter.

"Guess he needs a bit more encouragement." Shakey walked to the horse's left side and loudly slapped a palm atop his sleek rump.

Haygood's Lad didn't bat an eye.

"Careful there, Boss," Earlie warned. "He can kick if he takes a mind to."

Shakey ignored the jockey and turned to Chance. "I need you to lend me a hand."

Which was exactly what the trainer wanted. Positioning the gambler on the colt's right side, Shakey stepped back to the left. He reached out, stretching his arm behind the horse just below the animal's backside.

"Lock hands with me," Shakey directed the gambler.

He waited for Chance to comply. "Stay in close. He won't kick if you're in close."

Chance rolled his eyes. With his cheek pressed against the colt's rump, he couldn't get any closer.

"On three," the trainer said, "Earlie, you pull, and we'll push. One . . . two . . . three!"

Hand locked to his friend's, Chance strained with all his might. Haygood Lad's front legs moved forward, then his hand.

"That's it!" Shakey's words came in laborous grunts. "We've got him now. We've got him!"

Abruptly the colt rushed forward, sliding to the right as he did.

The sudden movement and the weight of the horse against the gambler's side cost him his footing. Chance released his friend's hand, his arms flailing the air for balance.

It didn't help. One moment he stumbled on the wooden gangplank, the next he tumbled into the cold waters of the Ohio River!

Spitting, coughing, and sputtering, he managed to keep his head above the water. A chorus of laughter rolled from the dock.

The loudest was Captain Bert Rooker, who roared, "Somebody toss him a bar of soap! Shouldn't let all that water go to waste!"

Chance held the curses that sought to push from his throat and wetly grinned up at the laughing faces that stared down at him. His unexpected bath was far from an auspicious beginning to a journey meant to save his riverboat!

TWELVE

Hastily jotting down an answer to Philip Duwayne's telegram, Chance then handed the message, estimating William Forrest's time of arrival in Baton Rouge with two prized horses, to the telegraph operator.

"Thirty words at a dime a word. That'll be three dollars, Mr. Forrest," the clerk announced and held out a hand after carefully tallying the message three times.

Chance passed the man three dollars and waited until he sat down and tapped out the answer to the attorney's wire on the telegraph key. A moment after the man completed his coded clicking, the key *clickety-clicked* several times on its own.

"That's it, Mr. Forrest. Message's been received downriver and will be relayed to Baton Rouge by the evening," the operator said. "Anything else I can do for you?"

"That should be it." Chance tipped his hat and walked to the telegram office door.

"Thank you, Mr. Forrest," the man called after the gambler as he stepped into the streets of St. Louis.

Chance smiled to himself when he turned and strode toward the river. He was almost—*almost*—used to being called William Forrest. By the time he and his companions made it to Baton Rouge the temporary name might fit as comfortably as his own.

Shakey, Earlie, and Del had all adjusted to the

104

change without a hitch. Only Bert Rooker displayed any difficulty in the transition.

On at least three times during their trip from Louisville to St. Louis, the captain had slipped and called him Chance. While the mistake only caused redcheeked embarrassment now, once back in Louisiana it could destroy the whole tapestry they had woven. Chance mentally noted to take Bert aside and discuss the matter with him once they were under way again.

That one catch in his plan did not lessen the gambler's smile. So far everything was running smoothly. Both Kentucky Rambler and Haygood's Lad seemed uneffected by their riverboat journey. During their twoday layover in St. Louis, Shakey and his men had been able to take the two colts out into the country and exercise them. Shakey had no complaints over their performance.

Philip Duwayne's wire was also encouraging. The lawyer's message had described Lewis Rapper as a fish just waiting to snap up the bait. Rapper had practically invited himself to Baton Rouge to meet William Forrest.

Chance's answer had instructed Philip and Katie to plan an appropriate, formal function to commemorate Forrest's arrival at his new home. Rapper, of course, was to head the guest list.

After that, if Rapper had been sufficiently primed, all the gambler had to do was to sit back and let the man make his move.

Chance frowned. What if Rapper didn't make a move? Chance's scheme called for Rapper to propose a race between his colt Legacy and Shakey's horses. The gambler would have to carefully consider an alternate plan to nudge Rapper along if the man hesitated—

something subtle that made it appear the race was Rapper's own idea.

There's no way that he'll refuse the rematch that I propose. The stakes will be too high! The smile returned to Chance's face.

"Now!"

The gambler's thoughts of the future evaporated as his head snapped up. Two men who approached on the sidewalk abruptly broke into a run. Before he could react, they slammed into him like charging rams.

Air rushed from Chance's lungs in a painful gush. Hands grabbed his arms, spun him around, and threw him into an alley that opened to the left. Stumbling, he managed to regain his balance only after his back collided with the cold, solid brick of the building's wall running the length of the alley.

"Okay boys, make this quick and clean. We ain't getting enough for an all day job!" This from the opposite end of the alley.

The gambler's head jerked around. Two men, led by a third with a shaved head, rushed at him. Grasped in their hands, each of the three carried bludgeons as thick as tree limbs. All looked as though they had used such weapons before and were only too willing to employ them again—on him!

"Let's take him!"

Chance's head whipped back to the left. The two who had originally rushed him charged again, obviously intent on restraining him for their club-bearing companions.

With no time to go for either his derringer or bellygun, Chance lunged to the right, shooting past the two. Simultaneously his arms snaked out, hands clamping around the closest man's collar. Twisting at the waist, he used the leverage of his upper torso to send the man sailing headfirst toward the wall.

The attacker's groan drowned out the thudding sound of his skull striking the brick. He staggered back from the impact and collapsed spread-eagle on the ground, unconscious or dead—Chance didn't know or care which. He had four other problems on his hands.

As the first of the two attackers spun about in wide-eyed amazement that the gambler had escaped the charge, Chance lashed out with a hard-thrown right that connected with the bridge of the man's nose.

He felt rather than heard the crush of bone beneath his fist. The second man went down screaming and clutching his face. Blood gushed in a crimson flow from his shattered nose.

Assured that two of the five were at least temporarily waylaid, he pivoted to face the three led by the man with the shaved head. With clubs hefted above their heads, they ran straight at him like angry bulls.

Standing his ground at the middle of the alley, Chance tugged the watch chain that disappeared into a vest pocket. A double-barreled .22 Wesson derringer popped from the pocket into his palm. As his right arm rose to take aim on the bald man, his thumb arched up and cocked the single hammer. The instant the bludgeon-wielding man was in range, the gambler squeezed the trigger.

Black powder exploded in a dark acrid cloud. Two dark holes, one beneath the other, purple rather than red, opened between the eyes of the lead man. His head jerked back as two slugs of sizzling lead burned their way into his brain. A split second later, in delayed reaction, his body followed his head, falling backwards to the ground, twitching spasmodically as life fled it.

The unexpected death of their companion brought the remaining ruffians to a stumbling halt. Their eyes shifted between the dead man and the still-standing gambler as though uncertain what to do next. Only moments ago there had been five of them against one. Now there were only two.

The shrill blast of a police whistle was the deciding factor. Throwing their clubs at the gambler, the two turned and ran.

Ducking beneath the hurling missiles, Chance freed the Colt tucked into the waistband beneath his vest. The pistol came up too slowly. Both men darted from the alley and disappeared onto the street beyond.

"What's going on here?" A man's voice demanded behind the gambler.

Lowering the Colt, Chance turned to face one of St. Louis's finest. "I was attacked. Two of them got away."

"Wait right here," the policeman ordered, then ran to the opposite end of the alley. There he surveyed the street before turning back to the gambler. "They're gone. Don't see hide nor hair of anything but a beer wagon."

Chance tucked the Colt back under his vest as the officer walked back down the alley to kneel beside the man with the shaved head. He leaned an ear to the man's chest, then looked up at the gambler and shook his head. "This one's dead."

Chance didn't mention that the two bullet holes between the dead man's eyes made that fact obvious. He simply watched as the policeman snapped handcuffs on the ruffian with the broken nose, then moved on to the first attacker the gambler had disposed of.

"This one's still alive," the officer said as he pushed to his feet. "Care to tell me what went on here?"

Chance shrugged. "I was attacked and I defended myself. Other than that, I'm not certain what happened. Maybe these two can shed some light on why they and their friends jumped me."

The policeman eyed him suspiciously a moment,

then finally nodded. "I'll get these two back to the station and see what they've got to say for themselves. It's the meat wagon for the other one."

Chance lit the third cigar in two hours. As he blew out the match, his attention returned to the sergeant who grilled the two who had so rudely maneuvered him into the alley ambush. In disgust, the sergeant turned to two officers standing behind the seated men.

"Take the scum away. They can play dumb all the way to the gallows for all I care." The sergeant waved the two prisoners away.

Roughly the officers jerked the men from their chairs and hauled them away to waiting cells.

"Well, you heard all of it, Mr. Sharpe." The sergeant sank heavily into the chair behind his desk. "If them two know any more, they ain't spillin' it. Hard cases them two. They've been arrested at least ten times in the last year. None of the charges even stuck. Same with their friend you left laid out cold back in the alley."

Chance nodded. The two had remained close-mouthed all through the interrogation. All they would say is that an unknown man had hired them to kill the gambler. Whether or not they knew the identity of the man, the sergeant had been unable to ascertain.

Like as not, they don't know his name, Chance realized. For men such as these, the only thing that mattered was that the price was right.

"What about you, Mr. Sharpe?" the sergeant continued. "You know of anyone wantin' to see you dead?"

The gambler shook his head. "A man of my profession has a way of ruffling feathers. But those are usually soothed at the poker table—one way or another."

The sergeant pursed his lips thoughtfully, then nodded. "If anyone happens to come to mind, I'd appreciate it if you'd pass the information on to me rather than going after him yourself. Other than that, I reckon as soon as you read and sign the affidavit the detective is drawing up, you can be on your way."

Chance thanked the sergeant and walked from the office. Outside, he finished the cigar before the detective produced a neat and tidy facsimile of the gambler's recounting of the alley ambush. After carefully reading the report, he signed his name on the appropriate line under the watchful eye of a notary public, who witnessed the document and stamped it.

"If we have any further need of you, we have your New Orleans and St. Louis addresses," the detective concluded, bidding the gambler a good day.

Once on the street, Chance checked his pocket watch. Only an hour remained before the side-wheeler *Harthill* pulled from the wharf with William Forrest and entourage. The only trouble was—William Forrest hadn't boarded yet.

He snapped the timepiece closed, hailed a passing hack, climbed in, and ordered the driver to take him to the river. As the cab jostled forward, the gambler sank back into the overstuffed, leather seat.

Twice, he reflected. On two occasions since leaving the Haygood farm, someone had tried to kill him. *Who?*

Lewis Rapper stood in the forefront of his thoughts. Chance shook the notion away. That would mean that the attorney had somehow learned of William Forrest and his scheme to win back the *Wild Card.*

He refused to consider that possibility: those who knew of Forrest's existence were trusted friends.

If not Rapper, then who? Chance cursed. There was no one who'd want to take his life.

Be that as it may, he realized, someone out there was trying to kill him!

THIRTEEN

Chance scanned the faces of the crowd gathered to greet the *Harthill* at Baton Rouge while he descended the stairs of the riverboat to its main deck. A frown creased his forehead. He saw neither Katie MacArt nor Philip Duwayne.

Has something gone wrong? Doubts flooded the gambler's mind as he crossed the gangplank to the wharf.

Perhaps his earlier dismissal of Lewis Rapper as his unknown would-be murderer had been wrong. The attorney might have uncovered the William Forrest scheme and somehow prevented Katie and Philip from warning him. The gambler's right hand rose to rest against the slight bulge of the Colt concealed beneath his vest.

No, he told himself. He was overreacting; the two attempts on his life had him on edge. There were a myriad of reasons his friends might be detained. The trouble was, he couldn't think of any. Both Philip and Katie were too meticulous not to foresee and avoid any delays this day.

The gambler's cool blue eyes surveyed the wharf and the crowd gathered there. No riflemen ready to gun him down: no gang of henchmen armed with clubs. Did his mysterious would-be killer have another plan up his sleeve?

"Mr. Forrest?" A voice softly inquired behind him. "Mr. Forrest?"

Chance turned to face a young black man in clean, but frayed livery of brown who stood clutching a tricorn in both hands. The gambler nodded. "I'm Forrest."

The man grinned. "I'm Joshua, and I'm supposed to fetch you to your carriage."

"Carriage?" He arched an eyebrow.

"Yes, sir. It's waiting right over there at the end of the wharf." Joshua pointed to a carriage with a driver in the same livery at the reins of two matched pairs of dappled grays.

"Did Mr. Duwayne send you?"

Joshua nodded and started toward the waiting coach. Chance followed two steps behind. He had wanted it well known that William Forrest was arriving in Baton Rouge, but Philip's ostentatious display was going overboard. A footman and driver dressed in livery had gone way too far!

"Where's Mr. Duwayne?" he asked as Joshua opened the coach's door and held it open for him.

"He's with my brother. They'll see to the horses and your men," an enticingly familiar feminine voice answered from the carriage's interior shadows. "I asked him for this time alone with you, William."

The furrows on Chance's brow smoothed and a broad grin spread across his face as Charlette Blasingame's beautiful face poked out of the open door. "Won't you join me?"

The gambler needed no further encouragement. He climbed into the carriage and moved to the midnight-tressed young woman's side when she patted a cushion to her right. Joshua closed the door, and climbed on behind the coach as the driver brought the team to life.

"This is a surprise," Chance said, neither his gaze

nor his tone concealing his pleasure in finding the
woman waiting for him. "I expected Philip or Katie."

"I know." Light filtered through the coach's open
windows, catching Charlette's jet eyes and setting them
flashing like gems. Her graceful hands smoothed imag-
ined wrinkles from the skirt of the white sundress she
wore. "I asked Philip for this time alone with you. I
realize there will be little opportunity for us to be together once you arrive at our home. You and your
friends have too much to accomplish in too short a
time."

Chance wanted to say that he would always be able
to make time for such an enchanting woman, but he
couldn't. She was right. After reaching the Blasingame
plantation, business would be the order of the day until
the *Wild Card* was his once again.

Charlette's gaze left the gambler and perused Baton
Rouge's streets as the carriage moved from the city
onto a country road. When she looked back, she said,
"I've something I must show you before I can say what
I have to say to you. The ride's pleasant and won't take
more than an hour or so. Can you spare the time?"

The gambler nodded. Shakey Haygood had no need
of him when it came to the horses. Philip and Charlette's brother Howard would see that Shakey and the
colts safely arrived at the plantation.

Charlette smiled and settled back in the seat.
Chance's gaze studied the delicate features of her face.
His eyes alighted on the redness of her full, sensual
lips.

The magic this woman had ignited within him during
a single night in the French Quarter flamed anew. He
wanted to take her in his arms and cover her mouth
with his own—to once again share what they had savored that night in his hotel room.

He suppressed the urge and sank into the coach's

cushions. Charlette had given no indication that her greeting him was anything other than that—a simple greeting. The night in his bed belonged to another man and woman. This was not the French Quarter, but Baton Rouge. Charlette Blasingame had a reputation to protect.

"Not much farther." Charlette pointed ahead to a narrow dirt road that forked to the left.

Moments later the driver reined onto the road. The farm fields outside disappeared as a heavy wood abruptly pushed toward the blue sky on each side of the carriage. Chance questioningly looked at the young woman.

"Our home is another mile down the main road. What I want to show you is only a short piece this way," Charlette said. She grinned playfully. "Don't worry, I'm not abducting you."

"The thought hadn't crossed my mind," he assured her, still unable to fathom what she wanted to show him that was so important.

"Whoa!" the driver outside called to the team. Slowly the carriage drew to a halt. Joshua was at the door again, opening it and calling in: "We're here, Miss Charlette."

Not waiting for Chance to climb from the coach and assist her down, the black-haired beauty stepped outside and looked up at the driver. "You and Joshua wait here until I return. I've something to show Mr. Forrest, and it may take some time."

Charlette turned to Chance as he exited the carriage. "It's over this way, down that path."

Taking his hand, she led him into the woods of pines, sweet gums, and live oaks. The path they traveled was barely discernible from the heavy-weeded undergrowth. Chance's puzzlement grew with each step.

"There, just over the creek." Charlette tilted her head

slightly to the right while she picked her way across five flat stepping-stones that pushed up from the shallow stream's bed. "This is what I wanted you to see."

Nestled in the shadow of five long-needled pines was a small log cabin. In spite of its obvious age, the structure appeared in perfect condition.

Chance glanced at his beautiful companion, still unable to understand why she had brought him here to this secluded cabin.

"It was my great-great-grandparents' home. They built it when they first came to this land," Charlette explained with unashamed pride. "My father restored it just before the war. I've kept it up ever since. It's become my special place. I often come here when I need to be alone, to think."

She turned to the gambler, taking his hand once again, guiding him to the cabin. "This says more about what I feel in my heart than I can ever put into words. For me it's a standing symbol of what this land means to the Blasingames. It's our history in this country. It *is* the Blasingames. We shaped it from wilderness, fought for it for five generations. We even managed to keep it during a war that set brother against brother. Without this land, we're nothing."

She opened the door and led Chance inside. The cabin was one single room. A stone hearth and a table were crowded to one side. A bed hewn from pine filled the other side of the room. A colorfully stitched quilt was neatly arranged atop a feather mattress. Two down pillows lay at the head of the bed.

"This is why I brought you here, Chance." Charlette's voice softened as she called him by name. "You had to see with your own eyes what this land means to Howard and me. Only then could you have a glimmering of how important what you've done for us is. You've allowed us to keep this."

"It was a good investment." Chance felt a twinge of embarrassment. "I expect the Blasingames will use the *Wild Card* for all their shipping. And I don't doubt that they'll be able to convince their neighbors to do the same."

"Don't make light of what you've done for Howard and me." Charlette's face lifted to his. "You've given us back our lives. You're a good man, Chance Sharpe."

The gambler didn't know what to say. How could he explain that goodness had nothing to do with his act? Fear was at the root of his decision—fear that someone as beautiful as Charlette Blasingame would be forced into a desperate marriage with a man the ilk of Lewis Rapper, just to save her family's land.

"That's why I brought you here, to say thank you in my own way." Charlette leaned to him and rose on her tiptoes to lightly kiss his lips.

Chance's arms rose to encircle her waist, but she stepped back, her dark gaze never leaving his blue eyes. "I've never brought anyone here with me before, Chance. Not even Howard. No one will disturb us."

Before the gambler could answer, the midnight-tressed woman tucked her long fingers beneath the right strap of her sundress to slip it over the gentle curve of her shoulder. Next came the left strap, leaving no doubt as to how she intended to say thank you.

While Chance discarded his coat and went to work on the pearl studs of his shirt, Charlette tugged the white dress down to her waist. Her breasts, heavy and slightly pendulous, swayed in a delightfully seductive dance. Nut-dark nipples poked aroused and erect into the air atop each of those creamy upthrust mounds.

Giving her hips a provocative wiggle, she let the dress fall to the floor. Chance smiled. She had come prepared for this moment, her body unencumbered by the usual layers of undergarments with which most women hid their femininity. Charlette toed the dress and the shoes she wore away to stand before him naked. There was no hint of shame in either her beckoning expression or the flash of her obsidian black eyes.

Shirt skinned away, Chance had to sit on the edge of the bed to tug away his boots, socks, and trousers. All the time, the young beauty's gaze caressed his body. When he was as naked as she, Charlette came to him.

With palms flat on his chest, she pressed him down atop the bed, her lips covering his, her tongue thrusting deeply into his mouth. A low, moaning groan pushed up from her throat when his own hands cupped the elongated, dangling forms of her breasts to knead the pliant mounds to his—and her—delight.

Having positioned him flat on his back, she straddled his waist on her knees. Her hands then slid down the muscle-rippled plain of his belly, moving even lower until she held him between her stroking, caressing fingertips. He grew, lengthened beneath the playful ministrations. Only then did she slip her mouth from his and sit straight above him.

Her dark eyes were those of a hungry predator, when she clasped him in a tight fist and pulled him straight into the air. As his gaze devoured her beauty, she rose on her knees, then slowly lowered herself, guiding him upward into the moist heat of her body.

The summery warmth of her buttocks resting atop his thighs, she rode him. In gentle circles her pelvis undulated, while his own hips thrust as best they could beneath her restraining weight.

Reaching up, he eased her forward so that she hung above him on outstretched arms. Tilting his head, he captured one of the dark cherries that so temptingly swayed just over his lips. A shuddering groan quaked through the sleekness of her body as his tongue laved around the swollen bud of flesh.

The undulation of her body grew with insistence when his hands once more possessed the silky warmth of her breasts. Husky moans transformed to lip-writhing groans of pleasure. He sensed her mounting desire that was equaled by the fiery pressure the gambler felt expanding in his own loins.

Releasing one of her breasts, he edged a hand between their cores. An inquisitive fingertip sought and found the moist, erect button of her pleasure. Gently he massaged, feeling shiver after desire-filled shiver shoot through her supple body.

With a throaty cry of pleasure fulfilled, she collapsed atop him, her arms no longer able to support her weight as her body released the passion it held. Clinging to her shuddering body, Chance allowed his own desire to erupt from his groin.

Gratefully, they clutched tightly to each other until the last trembly thrill drained from their bodies. When Charlette at last rolled from the gambler, it was not to rise and dress, but to pull him atop her.

More than the previously mentioned hour passed before they abandoned the simple pine-hewn bed to pick their way through the woods to the carriage that awaited them.

Howard Blasingame waved an arm at the twenty-stall, whitewashed stable. "I've ten horses, five brood mares, a stud, and the four grays you saw in harness. I was forced to sell the other ten over the past year."

Chance noted a hint of embarrassment in the young man's voice. At twenty-two, Howard had nothing of which to be ashamed. That he and Charlette had managed to keep their land in the chaos after the war was nothing short of a miracle.

"If these ten aren't enough, I can arrange for the loan of others from our neighbors," Howard suggested.

Chance looked at Shakey for advise.

The horse trainer shook his head. "With the two colts that makes twelve. If Rapper wonders about the empty stalls, we can tell him that your other horses will be shipped downriver as soon as Del or I can go back for them."

The gambler nodded his approval. After all, William Forrest was in the process of establishing a breeding farm. The empty stalls would indicate he was just beginning his work here in Baton Rouge. "What about a course for our races?"

"My father and some of the other landowners used to race," Howard said as they continued the tour of the Blasingame plantation. "There's a cleared strip about half a mile from the house."

"I've taken a look at it," Shakey added. "It needs mowing, but it should serve our purpose. I'll start the colts on it tomorrow morning."

"What about the colts?" Chance asked when they turned back to the white-columned Blasingame home. "Are they going to be ready for Rapper?"

"They appear to be fit as a fiddle," the trainer said. "The captain letting us take them off the boat for a little ride each night after we moored seems to have done the trick. Give me five days, and they'll be as ready to run as they were back home."

"What about the time, Philip?" Chance glanced at the young attorney.

"No problem. William Forrest's welcoming celebration is set for this weekend," Philip answered. "Just make sure you don't hold the first race until the next weekend."

Chance bit at his lower lip. The weekend was three days away. One race the week after that and the second the following weekend—that gave him one whole week to spare before the *Wild Card* was scheduled for auction. Seven days wasn't much breathing room in case anything went wrong, but it was all he had.

"You have Miss Charlette to thank for arranging your party." Katie MacArt smiled at the dark-haired woman walking beside her. "She's handled everything."

Charlette quickly outlined the plans she had made: "There'll be fifty guests, all from Baton Rouge, I thought it would be safer to keep the guest list limited to Baton Rouge friends rather than inviting folks up from New Orleans. It offers less chance for someone to recognize William Forrest's true identity."

"Except for Lewis Rapper?" Chance smiled at the red-haired bartender.

"Aye, he's been mine," Katie replied with disgust. "You couldn't keep the man away from here this weekend. He's done nothing but ask about your horses."

"What have you told him about your brother, Miss Forrest? We need to get our stories straight," the gambler said as they entered the spacious antebellum palace.

"As little as possible. Our mother died shortly after I was born. Father was killed in the war." Katie paused as though trying to remember all she had told Rapper. "That's about it. I was careful not to invent more than I could keep straight. Remember, you didn't tell us much before you left."

Chance shrugged. "I couldn't say more. I wasn't certain exactly what I was going to do until Shakey showed me his colts."

The gambler paused to examine a lavish ballroom Charlette led the group of friends into. He grinned. "It's perfect. I can imagine it filled with Baton Rouge's elite."

"Eating and drinking the best that money can buy,"

Charlette added with a wicked smile. "It's easy to plan the social event of the season, especially when I have someone else's money to spend."

"Speaking of money," Phillip spoke up, "there's been a change in Rapper's financial situation since you went upriver."

"Good or bad?" Chance's eyes widened with interest.

"Bad for him, good for us," the lawyer answered. "As of this morning he has exactly one thousand dollars spread thin in five different banks."

"A thousand?" Chance's surprise transformed into a pleased smile. "What happened?"

"Another of his East Coast deals," Philip answered. "The man invested almost every dollar he had in a merchant vessel sailing to China and India."

A thousand dollars! Chance's smile grew. Rapper was more vulnerable than before. The gambler's gaze moved over the faces of his friends. "Fate has heated our iron white-hot. Now it's up to us to strike!"

FOURTEEN

Chance's right arm dully ached by the time the last of William Forrest's guests walked down the receiving line. For the past two hours, the cream of Baton Rouge's society had paraded by their city's newcomer, vigorously pumping his hand and wishing him success in his new venture with honey-dripping words that had already begun to repeat themselves after the first five minutes.

During that eternity, the gambler repeatedly found himself scanning the grand ballroom, searching for Lewis Rapper's pale, skeletal form moving among the richly dressed men and women. Only the New Orleans attorney mattered; all the rest—the plantation, the dancing guests, the orchestra, the two tables lavishly piled with food and drink—were merely elaborate pieces of scenery arranged upon a stage for the lawyer.

Tonight, Chance was baiting the trap he had so meticulously constructed.

"You may now dance with me." Charlette Blasingame slipped her arm into his. "All your guests have arrived, Mr. Forrest. It's time to mingle."

Chance glanced at her and blinked.

"Forget about Rapper," she said under her breath while she smiled and nodded as she led him through the guests into the ballroom. "Quit worrying. Let Philip do his job. When the time arrives, he'll have the man ready."

He tried to do just that as he took the woman in his
arms and swirled around the dance floor. But even with
such an alluring and desirable temptress so very close,
he couldn't push Rapper from his thoughts. Nor did
champagne and food help. Unless everything went
without a hitch tonight, his scheming was for naught.

With Charlette ever at his side, the gambler went
through the motions required of William Forrest. He
smiled at plump matrons with their equally plump, eli-
gible daughters. He laughed at jokes with flat punch
lines. He listened and nodded gravely while landowners
spoke in low tones of the Yankee invaders.

All the while, Lewis Rapper remained at the forefront of his thoughts. Katie and Philip had assured him
that the man had eagerly sought an invitation to Forrest's new home. Yet, not once had the attorney sought
him out this evening. Had his friends overestimated the
man's interest, or was Rapper playing a game of his
own? Was he sizing up Forrest before making his own
move?

Two hours of painfully dull gaiety dragged by before
Philip Duwayne approached the gambler while he listened to four men discuss the ins and outs of Louisiana
politics.

"Could I interest you in a game of poker, William?"
the attorney inquired, sticking to his carefully rehearsed
role. "Three other gentlemen and myself are about to
slip into the library. One is a fellow attorney from New
Orleans, a Lewis Rapper, who has expressed an interest
in getting better acquainted with another horseman."

"Poker?" Chance replied in mock surprise, fully involved in his own role as William Forrest. "Philip, my
man, I could think of nothing—"

On cue, Charlette broke in. "Philip Duwayne, go on
with you. Tonight William belongs to his guests. If you
must gamble, then do so without William."

Chagrin on his face, Chance shrugged. "A gentleman shouldn't argue with a beautiful woman."

Philip answered with a sigh and look of disappointment before he turned and hastened to the library.

Charlette politely extricated the gambler from the long-winded political discussion and moved him back to the dance floor. A smile touched the gambler's lips when he took the woman into his arms again. Rapper was on the line. He'd give the man a half hour to worry about ever getting a chance to talk with William Forrest, then slip into the poker game.

Lewis Rapper's dark eyes gleamed from their sunken sockets as he spread three kings, a deuce, and five on the table. "Read 'em and weep."

"Too good for me." Chance folded his own hand—four eights—and dropped the cards facedown before him. "And the night has been far too expensive."

"And me," said Howard Blasingame.

Both Philip and Bert Rooker, posing as James Bitman, captain of the side-wheeler *James Bitman,* nodded in agreement.

In truth, none of Chance's three friends had lost a dime. The gambler's educated fingers had seen to that whenever the deal moved to him. Only he had lost, often discarding winning hands to ensure that Rapper won handily.

"My first night in Baton Rouge, and I lose twenty-five hundred dollars. Not an auspicious beginning in my new home, gentlemen." Chance pushed from the table, and tossed down the last of the bourbon in his glass. "I think it's time that I called it a night."

As he started toward the library door, Rapper called after him: "Mr. Forrest, would it be too bold to ask if I could rise early tomorrow and examine your stable?"

Chance glanced over a shoulder and smiled. "I would be delighted to show you around myself. In the morning, then." He tilted his head to the attorney, turned, and left the room.

Absolutely delighted. He grinned outside the library: Rapper had walked into the trap; now all the man had to do was take the bait!

"Pleased to meet you, Mr. Rapper." Shakey Haygood took the attorney's hand and shook it. "Is your interest in horses casual or do you race yourself?"

"Mostly casual," the attorney answered while he and Chance followed the trainer to the stable. "Although I've got a colt I've raced a bit."

Chance hid his amusement at Rapper's answer. He *knew* the attorney's horse's undefeated record.

"Well, you won't find much racing material here, at least not now," Shakey continued as he led Rapper down the shedrow, nodding to the stalls he passed. "Most of the stock we brought down with us is brood mares."

The gambler noted that Shakey had rearranged the Blasingame horses. The four gray carriage horses were now sprinkled between the mares' stalls. Separated, the matched pairs were far less obvious. There was no way the attorney could guess their true purpose.

"You didn't bring horses to race?" Disappointment twinged the lawyer's voice, and he glanced at Chance.

The gambler found it difficult to conceal his growing amusement. Philip and Katie had been correct in their evaluation of the man. Rapper was chomping at the bit to find a race for his colt Legacy.

"Brought one colt that seems to have managed the trip downriver well enough, a three-year-old named Kentucky Rambler." Chance specifically mentioned the horse by name at Philip's insistence. "Shakey, show Lewis the Rambler, would you?"

The trainer motioned to the next stall and waved an arm to the black horse inside. While Rapper peered in, Chance lifted a questioning eyebrow in Shakey's direction, uncertain whether it was Kentucky Rambler or Haygood's Lad they viewed. The former jockey nodded, indicating it was indeed Kentucky Rambler in the stall.

Chance smiled. Perhaps Philip was correct in insisting that Rapper must not be deceived verbally. That to remain up and up legally, the man must make the choice of which horse he wanted to race of his own free will. That the gambler and his friends muddied the situation surrounding that choice was totally another matter—one less likely to be proved in a court, should Rapper seek legal remedies.

"Has the Lad had his work out this morning?" Chance asked, continuing his verbal sidestepping.

"Not yet," Shakey replied. "I was just about to send him out for a work."

"Good." He turned to Rapper. "Would you care to watch the Lad?"

"If you wouldn't mind." The attorney barely contained the eagerness in his voice.

"Not at all. Might as well walk down to the course while Shakey saddles the colt." Chance motioned Rapper forward toward the straightaway course behind the stable.

"A beautiful place you have here," Rapper commented as they walked. "I didn't realize Charlette and Howard had an interest in racing."

"They used to, before their father's death. It was almost by magic that I learned this farm was up for sale. Quite luckily, I secured it." Chance was beginning to enjoy the double-meaning word game he played. The enjoyment was tripled knowing that Rapper's understanding of his sentences was totally different from his own.

Reaching the course, the two men stopped on its edge, then looked back to the barn. Earlie Sutton, astride a black colt, was already half way to their position.

"A handsome colt, William," Rapper said while he studied the animal's lines. "Is your Kentucky Rambler a sprinter or distance runner?"

"Kentucky Rambler is a distance runner," Chance replied with an inaudible sigh. Rapper's own question gave him an escape from an outright lie.

"Mornin', Mr. Forrest," Earlie said when he passed the two men. The young jockey learned forward in the saddle and patted his mount's broad, muscular neck. "The Lad's feeling his oats today. He's ready to run."

Earlie's comment made it perfectly clear that it was Haygood's Lad that walked onto the training course—at least, perfectly clear to Chance.

"Give him his head. Let him run full out." From the corner of an eye, the gambler saw Rapper slip a stopwatch from his trousers and palm it in his right hand.

Clock him as much as you want, you oily bastard, Chance thought. *William Forrest allows his guests to see only what he wants them to see!*

"How far are you working him today?" Rapper watched Earlie urge his mount into an easy lope as he moved away from them.

"A mile," Chance replied, pointing to a series of posts that Shakey had set along the course. "Each of those marks an eighth of a mile."

Rapper nodded, keeping his right arm close to his

body to hide the watch in his palm. Chance saw his thumb arch slightly, ready to click the timepiece to life.

"Earlie's pulling him up," the gambler said as the colt dropped into a lope. "He'll be working from a standing start today."

A mile down the straight course, the jockey eased his mount to a halt and reined him around. For several seconds he sat there, then his heels slammed down. The colt broke, bolting into a full run.

Not even Rapper's hand could muffle the click of the stopwatch. Chance ignored the sound. He wanted the attorney to see the time—it was essential that he saw!

Although he couldn't see the watch's face, Chance knew the times Haygood's Lad was turning—twenty-four at the quarter pole, forty-nine at the half mile, and one fifteen when he covered three-quarters of a mile. True to form, the three-year-old flagged after that, his speed dropping drastically as he covered the last quarter of a mile.

From the corner of an eye, Chance watched the mild surprise on Rapper's face transform into a sly smile. The man sensed easy prey for his own colt—which was exactly what the gambler wanted!

"A good workout, Earlie," Chance called to the jockey when he brought the colt back toward their position. Remembering Shakey's orders after breezing the colt, he added, "Take him back and cool him out for an hour. Make certain he doesn't drink too much too fast."

The jockey nodded and reined toward the stable.

"A fine horse." Rapper's right hand slipped the stopwatch back into his breeches.

"He's coming along," Chance replied with a satisfied nod. "There's better back in Kentucky, but I'll have to wait a piece before bringing them down. I got stung pretty heavily last night."

"The poker game?" The gambler could almost see the wheels turning in the attorney's mind as he spoke.

"An unexpected loss. At an inopportune time."

Rapper saw an opening and moved in for the kill: "If it caught you short, perhaps I can help out."

"No, no." He waved the man away. "It's kind of you to offer, Lewis, but we only met last night. Accepting a loan would be totally out of the question. Besides, it's not a matter of not having the money. It's simply that I must free it from other investments. Still, my new friend, I do appreciate the concern."

"It wasn't a loan that I spoke of," Rapper replied.

"Oh?" Chance's eyebrows rose.

"I was thinking along the lines of giving you the opportunity to win back the twenty-five hundred you lost last night," the lawyer continued.

The gambler shook his head. "Another poker game? Sorry, but—"

"A race," Rapper cut him short. He tilted his head toward Earlie astride Haygood's Lad. "That colt, against my Legacy."

Chance halted and stared at the man beside him, then looked back at the jockey and horse. "That colt?"

Rapper nodded.

"Against your horse?" Chance held back a smile. Again following Philip's advice, the gambler carefully phrased his questions, making certain that Rapper chose the horse he would race against.

"Next weekend, here, over this course for a mile," Rapper replied. "We'll make the stake another twenty-five hundred."

Sharpe rubbed a hand over his neck and began walking again. Cautiously, making certain he didn't appear too eager, he waited until they reached the barn again before agreeing to the wager.

"I'll have Legacy here by noon next Saturday." Rapper barely controlled the excitement in his voice. "Say we set the race for one in the afternoon."

"One sounds fine to me." Chance nodded. His own heart pounded in his chest. The attorney had snapped up the first piece of bait. A week from today, Chance would toss him a chunk of meat that would strangle him!

FIFTEEN

Chance stood outside the Blasingame home and watched Lewis Rapper approach with his colt and an entourage of friends and acquaintances who had accompanied him from New Orleans to witness today's race. Before the man could cross the neatly manicured lawn to confront the gambler, Shakey Haygood greeted him and directed the man to take his colt back to the stable and prepare for the match race.

"We'll see you in an hour!" Rapper called out, waving to the gambler, and then followed Shakey toward the barn.

"Whew," Chance said, releasing a sigh of relief when he turned back to the house's open doors. He owed Shakey; he'd no wish to meet with Rapper any more than absolutely necessary.

"Look at the bastard," Bert Rooker cursed as Chance entered a long hallway. "Acting like he just took the colt off a steamer. Does he think we're all fools? We've known about his horse being in Baton Rouge since it stepped onto the wharf last Monday!"

"It doesn't matter," the gambler replied. "Let him think he's gotten away with something. It'll make it easier after the race."

"Too bad the son of a bitch has to win today," said the young pilot Henri Tuojacque, who stood beside the captain.

Chance shrugged; there was nothing he could say.

Allowing Rapper's colt to win against Haygood's Lad was part of the trap he had constructed for the oily attorney. The man's confidence had to be inflated before the gambler threw the real challenge in his face.

"Are you certain that you never mentioned that today's race wouldn't be against Kentucky Rambler?" Philip Duwayne asked, worry lining his face. "It's important, Chance. It—"

"William," Chance corrected his friend. "Please be careful of that, Philip. Rapper is too close to trip up now."

"William," Philip conceded with an apologetic nod. "However, that doesn't change the importance of making certain you never mentioned that Rapper's colt would be running against Kentucky Rambler today. It's our only defense against a claim of fraud."

For the hundredth time in the past week, the gambler assured his friend that Rapper had selected the colt his own horse would face today. "I mentioned Kentucky Rambler only once. After that Shakey, Earlie, and I were very careful to make certain we referred to Haygood's Lad as 'the Lad'—very careful."

If Rapper believed his colt went up against Kentucky Rambler today, that was his mistake—the exact mistake Chance had carefully cultivated. Winning back the *Wild Card* depended on Rapper's believing his Legacy could beat Kentucky Rambler.

"You mentioned something about some new information on Rapper's financial situation, Philip," the gambler said to his lawyer.

Philip grinned. "I received another report from my investigators this morning. Rapper's investments took a turn for the worse. Last week he learned that his cargo ship went down in a storm off the coast of South America."

"We couldn't ask for better news." Chance smiled.

With the thousand he originally had in the bank and the twenty-five hundred he had won last weekend, Rapper had only three thousand five hundred in hard cash. "Unless you can tell us his home burned down and he owes a few thousand in back taxes."

"No such luck," Philip answered.

"Give me a day, and I can arrange for a fire," Bert suggested with obvious relish.

Chance laughed. "Tempting, but I don't believe it will be necessary. After the race, we'll set our hook so deep that Mr. Lewis Rapper will never be able to wiggle off."

"Speaking of the race, the ladies are waiting for us," Howard Blasingame put in, hastening down a long curving staircase to join the other men. "It's twelve thirty."

Chance motioned his friends toward the door. "Shall we go lose, gentlemen?"

Spectators crowded beneath a canvas awning that Howard Blasingame had raised beside the long race course. Chance's gaze moved over the faces around him, making certain that he did not recognize any of the twenty-five men and women Rapper had brought with him. The last thing he wanted was to run into someone who had sat across from him at a poker table.

Assured his William Forrest identity was secure, the gambler slipped an envelope containing the two-thousand-five-hundred-dollar wager from his coat pocket and handed it to Philip. "Here, take this to Rapper. He can choose a man to hold the money."

Philip nodded and wove through the crowd to find Rapper. Chance glanced at Charlette Blasingame who stood beside him, smiling.

"Nervous?" she asked, slipping her arm into his.

"Except for the herd of buffalo stampeding in my

stomach, I'm as perfectly calm as can be expected for a man who just threw away twenty-five hundred dollars." His attempted levity fell flat—too much could go wrong to make light of the situation.

"Everything will go just as you've planned," the midnight-tressed woman assured him, giving his hand a squeeze. "Nothing will go wrong."

The gambler wanted to believe her words, only he knew that no matter how carefully one planned, things could go awry. What if Philip slipped up again and called him by his name? What if Haygood's Lad suddenly decided that this would be the day he could run a mile? What if Rapper turned his back on the wager Chance intended to make after the race?

So many things to go wrong. Chance drew a steadying breath to edge aside the *what ifs*. It did nothing to relieve the steel springs that tautened within every muscle of his body. Only when the race was over and Rapper had agreed to another race would he be able to relax.

A round of applause that moved through the spectators brought the gambler from his dark reflections. He glanced around, uncertain what was happening. Charlette nudged his side and tilted her head to the right.

Down the path leading from stable to course came two horses with riders in the saddle. Rapper's Legacy, a massive sorrel colt, pranced in the lead. The jockey on his back wore a black cap with silks of red-and-black diamonds. He tilted his cap to the crowd as he moved out onto the course and urged the three-year-old into a gallop to warm up the animal for the race.

Earlie Sutton waved at the spectators as he followed Legacy onto the course. The young jockey wore a green cap and silks of the same shade.

Chance frowned. Racing silks were the one thing

that he had not thought of. Where had these come from?

"The silks are my family's," Charlette said in answer to his unspoken question. "Katie and I have been working on your colors, but we didn't get them completed in time. I hope you don't mind the Blasingame green."

"It looks beautiful." Chance gave his approval, thankful once again for Charlette's touch.

On the course, the two horses and riders had galloped a quarter mile from the crowd. They turned and began a gallop that would take them to the starting position a mile past the spectators in the opposite direction.

"Look at him, will you?" Katie MacArt stepped to Chance's right. Her emerald eyes shifted to Lewis Rapper. "He's already gloating, and the race hasn't even started."

"He's got a sure thing," Chance answered in a whisper. "And he damned well knows it."

Past the shaded crowd the horses and their jockeys moved. Down the long straightaway they moved. Only when they galloped beyond Shakey and Rapper's trainer, who stood a mile away, did the colts halt and turn back. The two men, who stood on opposite sides of the course, stretched a rope between them. The jockeys maneuvered their mounts to the rope.

"This is it," Charlette whispered.

A fraction of a second later, the rope fell. Both horses lunged forward in a frantic scramble of long, stretching legs.

Get a hold on him. Chance found himself silently urging on Earlie as Haygood's Lad broke a length on top.

The black colt held the same advantage when the two horses darted past the post that marked a quarter mile.

Nor had Rapper's Legacy gained so much as an inch as the half-mile pole was met.

A mumble of doubt moved through the attorney's friends, who were well aware of the chestnut colt's ability. Chance smiled, noticing that worry furrowed across Rapper's white brow. The man busied a fingertip over his waxed mustache.

The same length separated the two colts when Haygood's Lad reached the three-quarters pole. Then that invisible brick wall rose before the black horse. In three strides Legacy regained the lost length and nosed into the lead.

Mumbling doubt among Rapper's entourage transformed to cheers urging Legacy's rider on to the finish.

Chance felt a portion of the tension ease from his body. Today was *not* the day Haygood's Lad would decide to go a mile. The colt crossed the finish a full eight lengths behind his only opponent.

"Have you ever seen a horse like that?" Rapper elbowed his way through the crowd. He waved Chance twenty-five hundred dollars under the gambler's nose. "Admit he's the fastest thing on four legs that you've ever seen."

Chance threw himself into the role of William Forrest. He stiffened and glared at the attorney, but no word uttered from his lips.

A gloating grin spread across Rapper's face from one ear to the other. "What's wrong? Cat got your tongue?"

Still Chance remained quiet, his cool blue eyes never leaving the lawyer.

"Maybe he ain't sure about moving down here form Kentucky, Lew," one of Rapper's companions laughed. "Maybe Louisiana horses are a mite better than he expected."

"That's not it, is it?" Rapper slapped the gambler on

the shoulder. "You're not regretting moving here, are you?"

Chance remained silent, waiting, doing his best to appear a man barely containing a mounting rage.

"That isn't it, Lewis," said a blond woman in a yellow dress. "He just wants a rematch."

Rapper laughed. "Any day of the week. But I don't think William here is that foolish. He's already seen—"

"Next Saturday," Chance cut in finally. "Your colt Legacy against Kentucky Rambler."

From the corner of an eye, the gambler saw a smile touch the corners of Philip Duwayne's lips in response to Chance's wording.

"What?" Rapper jerked around, his eyes wide with surprise. "Did I hear you correctly?"

"You heard me," Chance answered, then repeated: "Your Legacy against Kentucky Rambler one week from today—that is, if you think your colt can go another mile."

"You're serious, aren't you?" Rapper's grin still remained on his narrow face, but there was doubt in his voice.

"Twenty thousand dollars serious," Chance answered without blinking his eyes. "The reputation of my stable is at stake here."

"Twenty thousand—" Rapper stumbled over his words and swallowed. His eyes darted from side to side; beads of sweat glistened on his forehead. "You're joking."

"Philip!" the gambler called to his friend.

Philip moved to Chance's side and extracted a white envelope from inside his coat.

The gambler took the envelope and passed it to Rapper. "There's your joke."

Tucking a finger beneath the flap, Rapper opened the envelope and stared at the twenty, crisp one-thousand-dollar bills within. "You're crazy—twenty thousand on a horse race?"

Chance chose his words carefully. He had to maneuver the New Orleans lawyer into a corner, make it impossible for him to back out without losing face in front of his friends. "Perhaps I misjudged you. No *man* would ever consider a contest between horses a joke, Mr. Rapper." Chance pulled the money from the attorney's hands and placed it in his pocket.

Rapper's jaw sagged an inch as he glared at the gambler.

His horse had won handily, and now this fool was offering him twenty thousand more. Chance could almost hear the man's thoughts.

"It's as I thought, I've misjudged you, mistaken you for a horseman." Chance pivoted and started back to the Blasingame house with Charlette still on his arm.

"Wait!" Rapper called after him.

He turned back and coldly said, "Yes?"

"I'll accept the bet, but there are some conditions you must agree to," Rapper replied.

"Conditions?" He arched a disapproving eyebrow.

"The race will be held in New Orleans next Saturday at one. We'll run on the road that skirts Lake Pontchartrain."

"Agreed," Chance answered.

"I'll match six thousand of your wager in cash and give you an IOU for the remainer should my colt lose," Rapper continued.

"Now *you* jest." Chance shook his head. "You're a man of property, Mr. Rapper. Surely you have something you can stand against my twenty thousand?"

"My land?" Rapper's head moved from side to side in refusal.

"Lew!" A man at the attorney's left urgently whispered in his ear.

A smile returned to Rapper's face when he looked back at the gambler. "There is something—a riverboat I intend to place on auction in two weeks. I hope to get at least twenty thousand for it."

"The title to the paddlewheeler against my twenty thousand?" Chance watched Rapper nod eagerly. "My attorney will draw up an agreement stating the conditions of our wager. You may select your own witnesses."

Chance held out his hand. Rapper grasped it and shook it with all his might.

Only after the dust of Rapper and his friends' leave-taking had settled, did Chance close the door and allow himself a self-satisfied smile. He turned back to his friends who waited inside the house.

"This gets filed with the parrish first thing Monday morning." Philip held up the witnessed agreement Rapper had signed, stating the conditions of a race to be held between his colt Legacy and Kentucky Rambler. "Thinking of this was a stroke of genius, Chance. It's hard to refute a legal document."

"Just trying to make things nice and tidy," he answered. The idea for the agreement had come to him out of the blue. The gambler glanced at Shakey Haygood. "What did you think of his colt?"

"He's good." The trainer pulled a stopwatch from his pocket and showed its face to his friend. "He turned a mile right at one forty-two. He'll give the Rambler a run."

"But not quite a fast enough run." Chance's smile widened to a grin of victory. Next Saturday Lewis Rapper would discover the trap he had stepped into today.

SIXTEEN

"Clear away back there," the first mate of *Darr Dare* shouted, waving to the roustabouts on the main deck of the stern-wheeler. "Stand aside. Make way."

Chance stood on the Baton Rouge wharf beside Shakey Haygood. To their left Del Taggart and Earlie Sutton kept a tight hold on the colt they waited to load on the riverboat for the short journey to New Orleans.

"Are you certain you have enough time to prepare Kentucky Rambler for the race once you get downriver?" The gambler's certainty of two days ago had faded into a web of entangling doubts. Having overcome a thousand obstacles that had separated him from Lewis Rapper, he now saw a thousand more barriers that might prevent him from winning back his *Wild Card.*

"If I don't, it's a little late to start worrying, isn't it?" The trainer glanced at his friend and smiled. "But four days should give both the Rambler and Earlie time to learn the course. They'll be ready for Rapper's colt come Saturday."

Chance nodded, but worry continued to line his brow.

"The horse is my concern." Shakey reached up and squeezed his old friend's shoulder. "You take care of all you've got on your hands, and I'll handle Kentucky Rambler."

Shakey was right, the gambler knew, but it was hard not to let small concerns grow into mountains of worry.

"All right, you there," the mate's voice drew Chance's attention back to the stern-wheeler. "Bring the horse aboard; we're ready for him."

Del Taggart gripped Kentucky Rambler's shank close to the halter and stepped toward the gangplank that led to the riverboat. The three-year-old stepped onto the boards and crossed to the deck without hesitation.

"We'll be pulling out in an hour," the mate called to Shakey. "Have yourself and your equipment aboard by then."

Shakey waved acknowledgment to the man, then looked back at Chance. "Guess I'd better get this tack and myself aboard."

"Philip Duwayne will meet you at the wharves in New Orleans," Chance said. "He's made arrangements to stable the colt near the lake. He'll take you and your men there."

"And you'll meet me at the Hotel Burgundy this evening," Shakey replied.

"The Hotel *Burr-GUN-dee,*" Chance corrected, giving the man the new Orleans pronunciation of the word. "If you say Burgundy, nobody will know what you're talking about."

"Tonight." Shakey grasped his friend's hand firmly, shook it, then lifted the saddle and bridle from the pier beside him.

The gambler watched while the horse trainer crossed the gangplank onto the riverboat, then moved toward the penned colt. Chance glanced at the side-wheeler moored to the dock directly behind the *Darr Dare.* With no more room remaining on the smaller craft, he had booked passage for Katie, Bert, Henri, and himself on the larger boat. The side-wheeler would begin its trip downriver eight hours after the *Darr Dare*.

Although he would have preferred being aboard the same boat as Shakey and the colt, there was nothing he could do about it. Turning, he began the long walk down the wharf to where the Blasingame carriage with its four grays awaited him.

Chance opened his suitcase atop the bed. He then walked to a chest of drawers and withdrew the shirts and socks neatly arranged there. As he turned back to carry the clothes to the waiting bag, the rap of knuckles on wood came from his bedroom door.

"Come in."

The door opened inward, and Charlette Blasingame stepped inside, closing the door behind her. "Need some help?"

"Just tossing these things into the suitcase," he replied. "But I wouldn't mind some company."

Charlette took the clothing from his hands and tidily deposited them into the open bag. When Chance extracted two suits from a closet, she also took those too and neatly folded them into the case, then closed it.

"I'm not exactly certain how I want to say this, Chance." She glanced at him while she buckled the restraining straps.

The gambler settled on the side of the bed and smiled up at the beautiful woman. "Usually the direct method is the easiest."

"I'm not even certain there is a direct way." She returned his smile. "Feelings are hard to put into words."

Placing the suitcase on the floor, she sank beside the gambler on the bed. Chance reached out and took her hand. Again she smiled at him.

"You're a man I could get used to, Chance Sharpe.

There *is* magic between us. I felt it that night in New Orleans, and I think you sensed it, too."

Chance's hand tightened around hers; he nodded.

"We're a lot alike, you and I. Perhaps too much alike." Charlette's eyes locked to his. "These past few days, having you so close, started me thinking what it would be like to have you here on a permanent basis. I must admit, on the surface, it's tempting."

"Charlette—" the gambler began.

The black-haired woman pressed a finger to his lips. "Shhhh. Let me finish. I don't want you saying anything that you'll regret later."

Chance remained quiet and nodded.

"Like I said, we're too much alike. I could see us together for a few months, a year at the most, then one of us would start missing our freedom," she said. "It wouldn't work, so I'm not even going to try and keep you here."

The gambler stared at the woman, surprised by the twinges of regret that suffused his chest. He had grown closer to Charlette than he realized until now. Returning here after facing Rapper in New Orleans would be easy.

"However, I wanted you to know that there will always be a place for you here—the log cabin," Charlette continued. "It belongs to you and me. If you ever need me, for whatever reason, I'll be there for you."

Lifting the woman's hand, he pressed it to his lips. When he released her fingers, his arms encircled her waist, drawing her close. Their mouths meeting, they sank back into the soft mattress beneath them. Although not the log cabin, they could make this bed theirs, at least for the next few hours.

Chance stepped from the house intent on walking to the stable to deliver Shakey's instructions for Haygood's Lad to the grooms. Once that was completed, he and his friends would ride into Baton Rouge to begin the final leg of their journey back to New Orleans.

As he reached the end of a twelve-foot privet hedge that line one side of the wide path that led to the stable, he halted abruptly. Something moved on the other side of the hedge. He turned and stared at a rider mounted astride a bay.

"Del?" Chance blinked up at Shakey's foreman. "What are you doing here? Has something gone wrong?"

The massively built man shook his head and grinned, an expression that held no trace of humor. "Nothing's wrong—that I can't take care of now."

Taggart shifted in the saddle; his right arm swung a Sharp's breechloader across the neck of his mount. The muzzle homed directly on the gambler's chest.

Chance's own right hand crept toward the slight bulge of the Colt tucked beneath his vest.

"Forget it!" Taggart ordered, his thumb cocking the single-rifle's hammer. "Unless you want me to open a hole in your heart?"

The gambler let his hand drop to his side. There was no way he could reach the pistol before the man pulled the trigger. "That's what you intend to do anyway, isn't it?"

"That's the general idea, but in my own time," Taggart answered.

Chance stared down the long, dark barrel, his mind racing, and his temples apound. The derringer tucked in his vest pocket and the stiletto nestled inside the top of his right boot were as inaccessible as the Colt while Taggart held the rifle on him.

"Why, Del?" Chance asked. "What's this all about?"

"You're a dumb son of a bitch, ain't you?" Taggart sucked at his teeth in disgust. "I thought you'd figured it out when you first saw me back in Kentucky. I saw recognition on your face."

"Then we have met before." Chance stared out of the corners of his eyes, seeking an avenue of escape—or a weapon. Neither presented itself.

"You two-bit Yankee piece of shit!" Crimson anger flushed Taggart's cheeks. The man's eyes narrowed dangerously. "You telling me that you don't remember me?"

Chance tensed, ready for the man to squeeze the trigger. He had to delay for time, lull Taggart until the man gave him an opening or until someone from the house noticed his predicament. "You were the gunman who ambushed us on the way to Louisville."

"I asked if you remembered me." Taggart jabbed the rifle barrel at the gambler. "Do you or don't you?"

"And you hired the men who jumped me in St. Louis," Chance continued. He had found the man behind the attempts on his life, but he still didn't know why.

"Damned right I was!" Taggart answered. "My brother's rifle is good, but you was too far away back in them oaks..."

Brother? An icy shiver slid up the gambler's spine. A dark memory buried at the back of his mind wiggled upward.

"Should've known better than trust someone else to do a job for me," Taggart went on. "Wasted twenty-five dollars on them men back in St. Louis. Should've taken you myself, but there was no way to get away from the colts, not without Shakey or Earlie noticin' I was gone."

"And now it doesn't matter?" Chance pressed, playing for more time while he silently cursed his own stupidity.

How had he not seen it before? Del looked so much

like his brother! Why hadn't he seen it until now? He answered himself: *Because you've tried to bury Andersonville—tried to forget the long nightmare.*

"Reckon it doesn't matter anymore," Taggart answered. "I can make it out West from here, and nobody'll be the wiser. Nobody'll ever know who killed you, except you."

"It won't work, Del. The others will put two and two together and come up with you." As long as Taggart answered him, he bought more time. "When they do, they'll hunt you down and bring you back to the gallows."

The gambler had only seen Taggart a few times while in the Confederate prison at Andersonville. It was his brother Zeke whom he had met and learned to hate as he had never hated in his life, before or since!

Both men had been Rebel guards at Andersonville. However, Zeke had overseen the gambler and the other ten men packed into a single, dark, filth-covered cell. Another man might find pleasure in a woman's arms; Zeke took his pleasure from pain—the pain of other men. With whip and club, he inflicted pain at every opportunity, relishing the anguished cries and screams he tore from his victims' throats.

Five men Chance had watched the monster in human form methodically transform to quivering, mindless things. Daily he worked on them—broken fingers, backs turned to pulp by the deep bite of the whip, arms gradually, torturously twisted until bone and joint parted. And when Zeke had drawn the last piteous cry from their lips, he killed them.

It was for those five that Chance had pressed a crudely made knife—one honed from the handle of a tin spoon against the prison's walls during countless nights —against Zeke's throat the night he escaped from Andersonville. And it was for those five that he had drawn the razored edge across Zeke's flesh, opening his neck from ear to ear.

"They might figure who done it, but they'll never catch me." Taggart chuckled. Like his grin, the sound held no trace of humor. "There's a lot of country between here and the Pacific Ocean for a man to hide in."

Chance still saw no one. He was running out of time. He had to do something—had to force Taggart to make a mistake.

"You're wrong, Del. My friends will track you down." He drew a steadying breath. It was now—or never. "They'll find you just like I found your brother Zeke. And they'll kill you the same way I killed him—the way men kill mad dogs!"

"You do remember!" Taggart's eyes widened, alive with an insane light. "That's good, tin horn. That's real good! 'Cause I didn't want to kill you without you knowing why you was dying."

Taggart's right arm stretched to its full length. Chance saw the man's muscles tense, ready to squeeze the trigger.

"Die, you brother-murdering son of a bitch!" Taggart roared.

The man's finger tightened around the rifle's trigger. Simultaneously, the gambler dived to the right. The thunderous blast of black powder exploded as the hammer fell. Lightning pain seared Chance's left shoulder.

Too late! The gambler realized he had moved too slowly. Taggart's bullet had missed his chest, but slammed into his shoulder—the same shoulder that erupted in a wave of white-hot agony when he hit the ground in a roll, intent on somersaulting to his feet. The shoulder refused to support his weight; he collapsed facedown.

"Bastard!" The metallic clink of an empty cartridge flying from the rifle punctuated Taggart's curse.

"You're not getting away from me again—not this time!"

Through the burning pain clouding his mind, Chance forced himself to move. Clawing his right hand under him, he tugged the Colt from beneath his waistband, then rolled to his right. His right arm jerked up and his forefinger squeezed the pistol's trigger. The Colt barked at the rider above him.

The belly-gun's sawed-off barrel was perfect for close range; it failed at distances beyond six feet. The gambler's shot went wild. Desperately, he fired again —with the same results. A third time he pulled the Colt's trigger.

Although the sizzling lead repeatedly flew wide of its target, the ear-deafening reports found a mark. Taggart's bay shied, sidling to the left. The Sharp's breechloader fell from the man's hands.

"Chance!" Bert Rooker's gravel voice shouted in horror from the house. Henri joined the captain. "You there! Stop!"

Taggart's head shot up, his gaze homing on the Blasingame home. "Damn it!" His eyes rolled down to Chance. "It ain't over—not by a long shot!"

With that he jerked the reins and wheeled the bay about. His heels lashed into the horse's side, urging it into a full run.

Chance lowered the Colt as the man disappeared behind the high hedge. The hollow sound of hooves striking the ground quickly faded as Taggart escaped.

"Chance!" Bert reached his side first, but before the man could kneel, Charlette pushed him aside.

"You're hurt!" Her dark eyes darted to the crimson stain that spread across the left shoulder of the gambler's shirt. She looked up and ordered, "Bert, Henri, carry him to the house."

* * *

Henri held out a clean shirt, while Charlette and Katie finished tying the bandage they had wrapped around Chance's shoulder. When the gambler reached for the shirt, Charlette slapped his hand away.

"You can get by just like you are until we get you in town and let a doctor look at this," she said.

"No need." Chance shook his head. "The bullet went right through. If it had hit anything vital, I'd be dead by now. The bleeding's stopped; I'll be all right. If I need a doctor, I'll see one in New Orleans."

"New Orleans?" Charlette stared at him in disbelief. "You're not thinking of traveling with this arm?"

"I've got to." He tried to rise from the wooden chair in which he sat, but Charlette edged him back down. He felt too drained to push past her. "Don't you understand? Taggart knows everything. If he gets to Rapper, all we've done will be ruined."

"Bert and I can handle Taggart," Henri said. "Or at least make sure he doesn't get to Rapper."

The young pilot explained that the captain and he would return to New Orleans as planned. There they and the rest of the *Wild Card's* crew would keep the attorney under surveillance night and day.

"He won't get by us," Bert assured his friend.

"I don't know." Chance bit at his lower lip dubiously.

"Besides, Charlette's right," Katie added. "A doctor needs to look at that shoulder before you go riding down the river."

"You can rest here a couple of days," Charlette said, her dark eyes pleading with the gambler. "You can book passage on another paddlewheeler as soon as you're strong enough to travel. If need be, I'll drive you to New Orleans in our carriage. I won't let you down."

"I can travel now," Chance insisted. He tried to stand and fell back to the chair, his legs refusing to support him. "Guess, I'm weaker than I thought." He looked at Bert, Henri, and Katie. "It's up to you to make certain Taggart doesn't get to Rapper."

"He won't," Bert answered. "It's our boat, too. Remember?"

Sharpe smiled meekly and nodded.

"Help me get him upstairs to his room," Charlette directed the two men. "Then you three had best be on your way. It's an hour's ride into town."

With Henri and Bert's support, the gambler managed to climb the long, curving stairs to his recently vacated bedroom. There, from a curtained window, with Charlette at his side, he watched his three friends depart for their journey to New Orleans.

I'm alive, he thought, trying to find a silver lining within the dark cloud that had descended around him. The thought didn't help. He couldn't shake the feeling that the long weeks of planning and work were about to come apart at the seams, and there was nothing he could do about it.

SEVENTEEN

Chance stepped from the Hotel Burgundy and paused to glance at the sky. Although the heavy rains that had pelted New Orleans throughout the night had stopped three hours ago, threatening thunderheads still rolled overhead.

"Chance!" Charlette Blasingame called to him from a hack that waited by the curb. "It's eleven o'clock; you said that you wanted to be at the lake by noon."

With a final survey of the moisture-laden clouds, he hastened to the cab. In spite of an aching stiff left arm, he climbed in without aid to seat himself beside his beautiful self-appointed nurse. Katie MacArt, still dressed as Katherine Forrest in a flowing dress of forest green silk, sat on Charlette's left.

"Howard and Philip?" the gambler asked, noticing that his friend and Charlette's brother were not in the cab.

"They went ahead to Lake Pontchartrain," Charlette answered, her eyes ablaze with a coy glint.

The same impish light flashed in Katie MacArt's emerald green eyes when she added, "They knew that we wanted to be alone with you."

Chance's gaze shifted between the two beauties, uncertain what was happening.

"We have a present for you." Charlette reached beneath the taxi's seat and pulled out a bundle wrapped in

151

brown paper that she placed on the gambler's lap. "Open it."

He did; a pleased smile slid over his lips as he examined the racing silks within. The material was sky blue except for a large white patch in the shape of a playing card that covered most of the back. Intricately embroidered on that card was the colorful image of a grinning harlequin—a joker!

"A wild card! Perfect!" He laughed and leaned over to kiss both women on their cheeks. "I had forgotten that you two were working on this. It's perfect! This will give Rapper something he'll never forget!"

Beaming grins of pleasure covered Katie and Charlette's faces. Tapping the ceiling of the cab, Chance called to the driver, "Move it, man! A friend of ours has an important engagement, and we must see that he's appropriately dressed!"

"Still no sign of him," Bert Rooker said with a shake of his head. "Henri and I both stood watch on Rapper's home last night, just to make certain there were no slipups. Taggart never showed his face."

Chance's gaze scanned the crowd gathered beside Lake Pontchartrain to watch today's race. If the vengeful brother wanted a perfect opportunity to strike, it was here and now while the gambler's attention was on the race. Yet, Taggart's face was nowhere to be found among the men and women waiting for Rapper's horse to claim an easy victory.

"He's not here," Henri Tuojacque said as though sensing what coursed through Chance's mind. "Bert has placed twenty men around the area just in case Taggart decides to make a move today."

"I don't think he will." Chance's gaze moved out over the watery surface of Lake Pontchartrain. In the distance he could see sheets of rain falling from the gray clouds. "When he tried to gun me down in Baton Rouge, he kept mentioning escaping to the West. There's too many people here for him to make a clean break."

"Still, the men will make certain he doesn't try something," Bert said.

"Believe me, I appreciate the precautions," Chance replied. "It's my neck he wants. Anything you and the crew can do to stop him from getting it, is gratefully accepted."

The gambler surveyed the crowd again. His gaze was drawn to the right; Shakey Haygood approached the expectant spectators. Chance watched his old friend's hesitant steps as he walked the length of the race course that Rapper had chosen along the Lake Pontchartrain Road.

Something's wrong! A hollowness churned within the gambler's stomach. He could see it on Shakey's face, the way the man repeatedly worried his fingers through his blond hair, the movement of his lips as though the trainer talked to himself.

"Shakey?" Chance prepared himself for the worst when the man reached his side. "Is something wrong with Kentucky Rambler?"

"The colt's never been in better form," the trainer replied. "It's this road."

"Road?" The gambler stared at his friend. "But Earlie and the Rambler have trained here for the past four days."

"It's not that." Shakey shook his head. "Look at all this mud. The Rambler's never run in the mud before."

"Never run in the mud?" Chance's eyes widened. "You mean that—"

"I have no idea how he'll perform," Shakey said, his head moving from side to side. "Some horses don't take to slop like this. They get a little mud in their faces, and they pull up. Refuse to run, no matter what a jock does. Nothing anyone can do, except make sure they don't run in the mud."

The bottom fell out of Chance's stomach. Twenty thousand dollars and the ownership of the *Wild Card* rode on this race, and from out of nowhere Shakey was telling him the colt he had staked his future on had never raced in the mud.

"Can you—"

Chance was cut short by Lewis Rapper, who edged to his side and pointed down the long stretch of open road. "They're about to start. Kiss your twenty thousand good-bye, William."

In the gray distance the gambler saw two men stretch a rope across the width of the road. Rapper's jockey reined the chestnut colt's chest to the line first. Earlie waited until his opponent was in position before moving beside him.

"Care to increase our bet?" Rapper grinned greedily at the gambler.

The abrupt drop of the rope was all that stopped Chance from upping the wager another ten thousand to spite the attorney.

Both horses broke even; Chance's pounding heart soared, then fell. Five strides later Kentucky Rambler dropped a full length behind the massive sorrel colt.

"Give him a chance." Shakey nudged his friend's side. "It's new to him. He's not certain what he's gotten into."

Neither was Chance. He stared in cold horror while he watched the black three-year-old drop farther back with each long stride Legacy took. Two lengths separated the horses and only a quarter of a mile had been covered.

A wave of amusement rolled through the crowd when Legacy passed the halfway point of the mile race still two easy lengths ahead of his sole challenger. To all, it was more than apparent that there was no contest.

To all except Shakey, who called out, "He's holding his ground! Now bring him on, Earlie. Bring him on!"

His friend's shouts sounded like wishful thinking to Chance. Earlie's hands moved up and down Kentucky Rambler's neck with each stride the colt took. Run as the horse did, he still remained two long lengths behind Legacy.

With a quarter of a mile between the two horses and the finish line, the crowd was loudly cheering on Rapper's colt. Chance simply stood and stared. His mind and his body felt numb, unable to accept that it all was to end like this. After all the intricate planning, all the—

"Here he comes! Look at him! Look at him!" Shakey shouted at the top of his lungs. "He's making his move! Look at him!"

Chance blinked; his temples pounded like runaway bass drums. Kentucky Rambler *was* making a move!

The black colt's strong, long legs seemed to double their speed. The ground between the two horses disappeared. With only an eighth of mile left to the race, the two colts fought neck and neck.

The battle was short-lived: Kentucky Rambler easily nosed past the unbeaten chestnut. Under Earlie's urging hands, a nose stretched to a head—a neck. A full half a length in front of Legacy, the black colt lunged across the finish line.

Katie and Charlette went wild! Their arms simultaneously flew around the gambler, joyously hugging him. Their lips smothered his face in a shower of kisses. Nor did they stop there. Shakey, Bert, and Henri all received an equal share of the women's open joy.

It was Philip who approached Rapper first. "I believe there's a matter of a riverboat title to attend to."

Glowering at his fellow attorney, then at Chance, Rapper signaled the man who held the race's stakes to him. "Give it to him."

"Your signature first," Philip insisted, flashing a wink at Chance as he produced a bottle of ink and pen from a coat pocket.

Using Henri's back for a brace, Rapper opened the title and hastily scratched out his name. When he finished, he shoved the document to Philip. "There. William Forrest is now the owner of the riverboat *Wild Card!*"

"Don't take it so hard. It was only a horse race," Philip said with a wide grin as he handed the title and the envelope containing the twenty thousand dollars to Chance. "I believe these belong to you, Chance."

"Chance?" Rapper's head jerked around. His eyes narrowed to slits as he glared at Chance.

"The name's Chance Sharpe." The gambler carefully deposited title and money inside his coat. "And I own the *Wild Card* again."

Rapper's eyes widened first in astonishment, then in open mirth. "I'm afraid not, Mr. Sharpe. That title is absolutely worthless. It names William Forrest as the owner of the riverboat. I'm not certain what exactly happened here today, but one thing I do know is that the *Wild Card* is still mine. That piece of paper is worthless!"

Philip spoke before Chance could utter a sound: "You *are* a bad loser, aren't you, Lewis? I think that if you'll check the records at the courthouse, you'll find that William Forrest does exist—as a going business concern with Chance Sharpe as its sole proprietor. Mr. Sharpe *does* own the *Wild Card.*"

"You bastards!" There was no mirth on Rapper's face now. "It will never stand up in court. You know that!"

"I believe it will," Chance answered. He looked at

Philip and returned his friend's earlier wink. "I have that on very sound legal authority."

"We'll see, Mr. Chance Sharpe. The *Wild Card* is mine, and I damned well intend to keep it." Rapper spun to face Philip. "And we'll see *you* in court!"

The attorney pivoted sharply and pushed his way through the crowd to where his carriage waited.

"He *is* a bad loser!" Henri whistled softly. "The man is just looking for a fight."

"Exactly my thoughts. And not just in the courtroom." Chance's mind raced; Rapper had more than legal maneuvers up his sleeve. "Bert, you've got two hours to gather the *Wild Card's* crew and get them aboard our boat."

"They'll be there," the captain answered without hesitation.

"Chance?" Charlette reached out and took his arm. "Is there something wrong?"

"Maybe not," the gambler tried to reassure her. "But now that the *Wild Card* is mine again, I just want to make certain Rapper keeps his hands off her!"

"Chance, we've got company." Henri pointed to the head of the wharf.

Chance turned and grasped the rail of the *Wild Card's* boiler deck. The minor repairs the riverboat needed after two months of neglect were immediately forgotten. A small army of men armed with clubs marched down the long pier toward the riverboat.

"Looks like Galt Ferris and his gang," Henri said. "Rapper *did* have more than a court battle in mind."

"I was hoping he'd show up again." Bert smiled. "I still owe him a thing or two."

Chance estimated the force that marched on the *Wild Card* as forty men. "Okay, this is it. Henri, get Katie and the rest of the women off the boat. There's no need

for them getting involved in this. Bert, get the crew
onto the dock. I don't want one of Rapper's men setting
foot on my boat."

As the captain started toward the stairs that led to the
main deck, Chance called after him. "Clubs only, Bert.
No knives, axes, or guns. This will be a fair fight."

"What about you?" Henri asked. "That arm hasn't
healed yet."

"You worry about getting the women off the boat.
I'll worry about my left arm," he snapped. "Now get a
move on. I don't want any of the women hurt."

Offering no further argument, Henri darted into the
main saloon. Chance moved down to the main deck,
where he ducked into the boiler room. A hasty search
of the cords of wood stacked there produced a three-
foot oak limb tapered at one end so that it fit snuggly
into the gambler's good right hand.

Hefting the bludgeon, he walked outside and crossed
the gangplank. Behind him Bert and thirty members of
the *Wild Card's* crew, armed with everything from broken boards to skillets liberated from the boat's galley,
spread in a line along the wharf.

Down the pier, Galt Ferris and his gang of hired
toughs fanned out. Rapper, who preferred to do his
dirty work in the courts, was nowhere in sight.

"That's far enough," Chance shouted when the men
were twenty feet from his position. "You can turn
around and go home. Rapper has no claim to this boat
now."

"That's not the way he tells it," answered a barrel-
chested man with a black beard sprouted thick as a coal
pile over his cheeks and chin. "Get 'em, boys!"

Clubs raised and ready, Rapper's men charged.

"Step aside!" Bert Rooker shot in front of Chance.
"The one with the beard's Galt Ferris, and he's mine!"

The captain, carrying a three-foot piece of oak limb

of his own, blocked an overhead swipe from the gang's leader. At the same time he lashed out with his right leg, burying a booted foot in the man's groin. Ferris doubled over, clutching himself.

That was all Chance saw, his attention rudely diverted by a red-haired man fully intent on splitting his skull with the bludgeon he wielded. Ducking beneath the whistling club, the gambler swung the length of oak upward. With a loud crack, it connected solidly with his attacker's chin.

Stunned, the man's head jerked back. The gambler's wrist flicked; the oak branch flipped three hundred and sixty degrees to slam down directly atop the man's mop of red hair, sending him to the wharf with a bestial grunt.

Twisting to the left, Chance used his one-handed grip on the oak branch to block a blow delivered by a man in a green plaid shirt. The gambler took Bert's lead and slashed out to drive a boot into the man's crotch.

When his attacker staggered back, Chance flicked his wrist again, spinning his club up and then down atop green-plaid's head. Like the first, he fell to the wharf, his eyes rolling back in his head.

The gambler wasn't quick enough for the third man who rushed him. Searing pain exploded along Sharp's right side when a club slammed heavily into his ribs. Dropping to a knee beneath the impact, he groaned and gasped to recover the wind that had been driven from his lungs—and barely managed to lift the length of oak to deflect an overhead blow meant to split his skull open like a ripe melon.

Pushing back to his feet, Chance stumbled to the side to dodge another blow meant for his pain-throbbing ribs. At the same time, his right arm jerked up and slashed the oak limb into his third attacker's left temple. The man swayed under the blow, then toppled forward like a felled pine when a club appeared out of nowhere and cracked atop his head.

Standing behind the fallen man, Bert grinned up at Chance and winked. "Only fair. You've just got one good arm!"

The captain spun about, ready to meet a new attack. None came. Half of Galt Ferris's gang lay groaning on the wharf. The other half ran from the *Wild Card's* howling crew who chased them from the river. As quickly as it had begun, it was over!

Chance heaved a sigh of relief, his eyes surveying the fallen men. "Bert, if any of these are ours, see that their injuries are treated. As for the others, pile them together and call the police. It's Rapper's turn to bail his men out of jail!"

EIGHTEEN

Chance entered the Hotel Burgundy's casino with Charlette Blasingame on his arm. The gambler's gaze surveyed the spacious room; a pleased smile lifted the corners of his mouth.

"Are you certain that you're not tempting fate a bit?" The woman's dark eyes shifted up to Chance. "After all, the last time you and the *Wild Card's* crew celebrated here, you lost your riverboat."

"Two months ago I didn't know about a man named Lewis Rapper. I was working with a blind side." He squeezed the woman's hand in reassurance. He tilted his head to a table on the right. "There're the others."

Bert, Henri, Shakey, and Katie sat together, each with a champagne glass in hand. Judging by the empty bottle on the table and another that was halfway to the same condition, Chance realized that the four were well into their celebrating.

Crossing the casino did bring a shiver of doubt to the gambler. Charlette was right; it was here, following his own release from jail, that things had collapsed about his head two months ago.

No, he told himself, a bolt of lightning named Rapper had already struck and spent his last spark in a New Orlean's court. The shady attorney had nothing left with which to strike again—Philip Duwayne had ably seen to that during this past week.

When the gambler and the dark-haired enchantress

on his arm reached the table, Katie poured two additional glasses and passed them to the latecomers. She then lifted her own drink in a toast. "To the *Wild Card*, now that she is at last legally ours again!"

No one refused to drain their glasses, nor did they wave away the next round that Henri poured.

"Has anyone seen or heard from Philip?" Chance asked, watching the others shake their heads. "He said he'd meet us here."

"To the two damned finest horses in this country—Haygood's Lad and Kentucky Rambler," Bert proposed in slightly thick-tongued words. "And to Shakey Haygood, the greatest horse trainer ever to walk this green earth!"

Shakey laughed and clinked his glass against the captain's. "I'm not a modest man, so I'll accept that astute evaluation of my abilities. But I think that you should also include Earlie. The boy's a hell of a rider."

"Yeah." Bert nodded and grinned. "To Earlie too!" Then he inhaled the contents of his glass in one gulp. "Where is the little lad? He should be here with us."

"The boy's only fifteen and has a strict ma and pa back home," Shakey replied. "For the sake of my horses and his backside, I decided that he wasn't quite ready for the French Quarter."

Charlette's elbow nudged Chance's side. "There's Philip."

The gambler glanced to the casino's entrance and waved the young attorney to the table. Only after he had downed a glass of champagne did his friends allow him to explain the broad grin plastered across his face.

"I just saw Lewis Rapper on his way back home to Washington, D.C.," the lawyer announced proudly.

Chance's eyes widened. "He's left New Orleans?"

"On a merchant ship—it was all he could afford." Philip sipped from a fresh glass of wine. "We left him with the clothes on his back and about ten dollars in his pocket."

"Left him with too much," Bert grunted. "That he's still alive is too damned much for the whoreson." Embarrassment spread over the captain's face, and he sheepishly glanced at Katie and Charlette. "You ladies excuse my grammar."

"It's not the first time anyone at this table has heard your curses." Katie reached out in a daughterly gesture and patted the man's hand. "Nor do I think it will be the last."

"Ten dollars?" Shakey's brow furrowed. "I thought Rapper was better-heeled than that."

"He was, but the parrish auctioned his personal property today," Philip replied, that self-pleased grin still spread from ear to ear. "By the time we and the rest of his creditors were through with him, he barely had the money for his ticket back East."

The attorney paused to reach in his coat and pull out two bulky envelopes stuffed to the seams. He passed them to Chance. "This is your share—minus my fees, of course. All in all, it covers your expenses plus about five thousand."

The gambler hefted the envelopes in a hand, enjoying their weighty feel. Not only had he gotten his riverboat back, but he had increased his bankroll to boot. *Not bad,* he thought. *Not bad at all!*

"Ten dollars in his pocket and the clothes on his back!"

Chance raised his glass to the lawyer. "Philip, my friend, you have a mean streak hidden beneath that gentleman's exterior that I greatly admire!"

True to his threat, Rapper had filed suit alleging fraud in the race between his colt and Kentucky Rambler. To Chance's surprise, the man had presented accurate details of how the gambler had switched horses on him.

Del Taggart? Chance wondered, realizing that the man must have been involved somehow, although he never once appeared during the three-day court case. After three failed attempts on the gambler's life, Taggart seemed to have given up and vanished. For that, Chance was grateful; a man couldn't live with one eye constantly cast over his shoulder.

No matter how accurate the details, Philip's careful planning parried his every maneuver with Shakey, Earlie, and the gambler as they were called to testify. When Rapper took the stand to provide his own version of what had occurred, Philip shredded his story into pieces before the jury. Under cross-examination Rapper admitted that he had indeed chosen Haygood's Lad to go against his colt in the first race.

The crowning touch of the case, Chance admitted with no lack of pride, was the witnessed agreement Rapper and he had signed. The hard evidence in black and white was all the jury needed to dismiss Rapper's claims and uphold the title transfer.

For Chance, that would have been enough. It wasn't for Philip! He countersued, alleging that Rapper's false claims were no more than malicious slander, designed to destroy the gambler's reputation. The jurors agreed; the heavy damages they had awarded were now in Chance's hand.

Opening one of the envelopes, he extracted eleven one-thousand-dollar bills. He handed five to Shakey. "This is what I promised when the two races were run." He then passed another five to his friend. "And the five thousand bonus." Finally he gave the trainer the remaining bill. "That is for Earlie. I believe it's customary to stake a jockey after he's won a race."

"Earlie will appreciate it," Shakey replied while he

carefully placed the money deep within an inside pocket of his coat. "And I *do* appreciate it. Chance, if you ever decide to go into the horse business, get in touch with me. We'd make one hell of a team! I'm going to miss working with you. In fact, I'm going to miss all of you."

"We've kinda gotten used to you, too." Bert's voice grew more slurred with each mouthful of champagne he swallowed. He reached out and slapped the trainer on the back.

Shakey tugged a watch from his vest and thumbed it open. He shook his head. "I'm afraid that the missing is going to start right now—my steamer leaves in another hour. I have to be going."

"Charlette and I will go with you to the wharf," Chance said as he pushed from the table.

A pleased smile touched Charlette's red lips, and her jet eyes flashed with understanding. Another riverboat would be returning her to Baton Rouge tomorrow morning. As soon as they returned from seeing Shakey on his way back home, they would begin a more private celebration of their own.

"It's been exciting, Chance." Earlie shook the gambler's hand. "Never been out of Kentucky before now."

Chance smiled and watched the young jockey turn to board the side-wheeler *Hutchin's Pride*. With a last wave to the dock, Earlie hastened to the stall at the steamer's prow where Kentucky Rambler waited.

"It *has* been exciting," Shakey agreed when he grasped his old friend's hand in that viselike grip. "I meant it when I said I was willing to go partners with you, if you ever decide to give racing a try."

"I know," Chance replied. "But right now, I've got my hands full with a riverboat."

"Maybe one day, Chance." Shakey nodded, then said his farewells to Charlette.

"Maybe one day," the gambler repeated as he watched the trainer cross the gangplank onto the paddlewheeler's main deck.

Moments later roustabouts freed the *Hutchin's Pride's* mooring lines. One of the monstrous paddlewheels came to life, lazily swinging the boat out into currents of the Mississippi River. Bathed in the light of a full moon, the steamer nosed upriver with both big wheels churning the water to frothy foam.

His arm around Charlette's waist, Chance stood watching the riverboat disappear around a curve in the river. He could not ignore the sense of loss that suffused him. Shakey was an old friend; he would be missed.

"You're lucky to have a friend like that." Charlette rested her head on his shoulder.

Chance eased her around until she faced him. He then lifted her chin with a finger and lightly kissed her lips. "That's not all luck has brought me."

She returned the kiss; a familiar hungry gleam flashed in her dark eyes. "Is there any reason we're standing here?"

"None—none at all!" He tucked her arm in his and walked toward the cab that waited for them at the head of the wharf.

The gambler's eyes narrowed as they reached the hack—the cabby no longer sat on the driver's seat. Chance glanced around, unable to find the man or shake the uneasy sensation that something was amiss.

"Wait here." He placed Charlette beside the taxi's door. "I'll see if I can find where our driver has disappeared."

Edging around the cab, he found the missing man—sprawled on the ground. Dropping to a knee, the gam-

bler felt the man's neck and found a pulse—he still
lived!

Reflected moonlight glistened from a dark, moist
spot on the side of the driver's head. Gingerly the gambler reached out and touched a lump protruding from
the man's skull. Moisture, sticky and warm, covered
his fingertips.

Blood! Chance's gaze shot around, searching the
night's shadows. Someone had hit him—hit him hard!

"Chance!" Charlette called out, her voice tight and
strained. "Chance!"

Standing, the gambler moved back around the cab
and froze! An icy shiver coursed along his spine.
Chance found the cabby's unseen assailant—Del Taggart!

"Told you it wasn't through, you bastard." A cold
grin contorted the avenging brother's face.

Chance remained motionless, temples pounding and
mouth gone dry. Taggart held Charlette with one massive arm looped about her slender waist. His right hand
clutched a hunting knife, pressing its six-inch blade
against the whiteness of the woman's throat.

"It's you I want, not her," Taggart said in a voice as
cold as his grin. "Do what I say, and she won't get
hurt. Understand?"

"Understood." He nodded in reluctant acceptance.

"Good, good." Taggart's head tilted toward the gambler's waist. "First toss down that stubby, little belly-
gun hidden under your vest. Then throw away the
derringer in your pocket."

With no sudden moves, Chance carefully eased the
Colt from his waistband. The possibility of swinging
the pistol up and firing into Taggart's face pushed into
his mind. He discarded the idea immediately. The man
held Charlette too closely, using her as a shield. Although his head presented an easy target, the gambler's

sawed-off forty-four was too unreliable. Ten feet separated him from his would-be killer. At that distance the Colt's bullet could go wild and strike Charlette.

Taggart's blade was enough threat to the woman; he refused to risk a shot. Chance tossed the weapon aside. The pistol hit the ground and careened into the shadows.

"That's it." Taggart's grin widened. "Now the derringer."

The palm gun was even less accurate than the Colt. Chance pulled it from his vest pocket by its watch chain and threw it away. The only weapon remaining to him was the stiletto sheathed in his right boot. There was no way he could reach the blade before Taggart used his own.

"Now come over this way," Taggart ordered.

"You said you'd let her go." Chance didn't move.

"I said I wouldn't hurt her as long as you did what I said." Viciousness seethed in the man's tone. "Now, get over here. I don't want you turning tail and running."

In two strides the gambler covered six of the ten feet separating him from Taggart. He stopped again and stared at the man. "You've got me, let her go."

"Whatever you want!"

Taggart's left arm uncoiled from Charlette's waist. Firmly grasping her right arm with his left hand, he hurled her away. Charlette spun dizzily back onto the wharf as she stumbled to retain her footing and failed. With a cry of alarm, she collapsed in a heap on the ground out of harm's way.

And was forgotten as Taggart lunged forward. The long-bladed knife slashed out, driving for Chance's belly.

The gambler leaped to the right. Although he avoided the shining length of steel, Taggart's body slammed into his left side. Pain awoke in a blaze of hot agony. The still-healing bullet wound reopened, warm blood seeped down Chance's chest.

Grinding his teeth and fighting past the pulsing fire in his shoulder, he lunged to the left when Taggart twisted around and lashed out with the knife again. Nor did the gambler have time to try for the knife tucked in his boot.

Taggart moved with a speed that belied his muscular size. Like a raging bear he attacked and struck with the silvered knife again. And again. And again. The honed edge whispered through the night, slashing into empty air as Chance bobbed from side to side to avoid an untimely end to the fight—and his life.

"Dance around all you want." Taggart's words hissed between gritted teeth. "Won't do you no good. You're hurtin'; I can see the blood. You're gettin' tired."

Chance heard truth in the words. He was losing too much blood. The front of his shirt clung wet and sticky to his chest from the warm flow oozing from the re-opened bullet wound. The dangerous waltz they danced would soon end as his senses numbed and his reaction time slowed. The honed tip of Taggart's blade would dart slightly quicker than his tiring body, and he would die.

Unless he did something—fast!

Taggart lunged again, the long knife thrust straight toward Chance's gut. The gambler shifted to the left, letting the blade flash past him but a fraction of an inch from his side. At the same time, he struck. His fist balled to a hammer of flesh and bone, Chance slammed his blow full force into Taggart's midriff.

Another man would have doubled over, breath driven from his lungs by the solid impact. Taggart merely grunted as Chance's fist bounced off the heavy muscles corded over his stomach. In the blinking of an eye, he pivoted and threw himself atop the gambler.

Twist as he did, Chance could not escape the man's overwhelming bulk. He fell, his right hand barely managing to clamp around Taggart's right wrist and divert the blade that drove toward his face.

Together they hit the ground, Taggart's crushing weight fully atop the gambler, pinning him to the hard street. Beside his left ear, Chance heard a snapping crack; the blade drove into the brick-paved street with such force that the tip sank into the stone and broke off.

Tip or not, the knife remained deadly as long as Taggart wielded it. Chance writhed and rolled in a struggle to wiggle from beneath the man's confining weight. It didn't help; Taggart straddled the gambler, his knees clamped around Chance's waist, refusing to lose their seat.

"Gonna kill you just like you killed my brother." Victory flared in the man's eyes as he glared down at the gambler, his hot breath washing over Chance's face. "Gonna open your throat from ear to ear!"

Taggart's right arm began to rise. In spite of the blazing pain in his shoulder, Chance's left hand joined his right to clamp about the man's right wrist. Taggart's arm continued to rise as though the gambler were no more than a child clinging to him. The razor-honed blade gradually edged toward Chance's vulnerable throat.

Recognizing the futility of matching his strength against the iron muscles of the man seated atop him, Chance switched strategies. He attacked from the rear. The gambler jerked his legs up with all the strength in his body. His knees slammed into Taggart's lower back in a hammering double kidney blow.

Taggart howled; his body bolted upright. In that instant, Chance pushed him to the left with his arms and rolled to the right. Taggart, still stunned, tumbled from his seat. Desperately, Chance's right hand reached down, tugged his pants cuff up, and clasped the ivory-handled stiletto nestled inside his right boot.

The blade flashed up just as Taggart launched himself again. The gambler saw a spark of horrible recognition in the man's eyes. A split second later Taggart fell atop his would-be victim, impaling himself on a slim blade that slid between his ribs and skewered into his heart.

Chance felt the man's body stiffen, then go limp atop him as life fled his massive hulk. Drawing two deep breaths, the gambler gathered the strength to shove the dead man aside and stand on rubbery legs. He stared down on Taggart's unmoving body, his mind uncertain whether to believe his eyes.

"Chance!" Charlette ran to him. Tears flowed down her cheeks and her words came between trembly sobs. "You're alive. You're alive!"

"Yes." His answer was less than steady. He still couldn't believe he had managed to survive. Hugging the woman close, he stroked her head, trying to quiet her quaking fear. "It's over. It's all over now."

The words were for himself as much as her. It was over, he tried to convince himself. Rapper had returned to the East, the *Wild Card* was his, and Del Taggart no longer threatened his life.

"Everything's all right. It's over." His arm tightened around Charlette, and he gently kissed her head.

He lied. Taggart was dead, but that was all. Nothing had ended. The wounds and hate left from a war that set brother against brother were still very much alive, still festered in men's guts. Only when both were dim memories of a half-forgotten past would it ever be over.

Until then, he and others like Charlette Blasingame and her brother Howard would survive and somehow rebuild a life for themselves out of the South's ashes as best they could.

"Come," Chance whispered, and turned Charlette from Taggart's still body. They walked toward the French Quarter's lights to salvage what remained of the night.